Praise for Amanda Young's *Missing In Action*

"Amanda writes with a dark sensuality that entices you to read long into the night."
~ *Nancy Lindquist, Author of How To Conjure A Man*

4.5 Nymphs "Missing in Action is a wonderful paranormal adventure filled to the brim with action. Sara finds herself surrounded by big, sexy men and makes some delicious choices as the story unfolds. Ms. Young pens a thoroughly entertaining tale with equal parts romance, paranormal and scorching love scenes. Without a doubt an author to watch for, and judging by this first book MIA promises to be a great series."
~ *Reviewed by Water Nymph for Literary Nymphs*

Missing In Action

Amanda Young

A Samhain Publishing, Ltd. publication.

Samhain Publishing, Ltd.
512 Forest Lake Drive
Warner Robins, GA 31093
www.samhainpublishing.com

Missing In Action
Copyright © 2007 by Amanda Young
Print ISBN: 1-59998-637-X
Digital ISBN: 1-59998-442-3

Editing by Sasha Knight
Cover by Vanessa Hawthorne

This book is a work of fiction. The names, characters, places, and incidents are products of the writer's imagination or have been used fictitiously and are not to be construed as real. Any resemblance to persons, living or dead, actual events, locale or organizations is entirely coincidental.

All Rights Are Reserved. No part of this book may be used or reproduced in any manner whatsoever without written permission, except in the case of brief quotations embodied in critical articles and reviews.

First Samhain Publishing, Ltd. electronic publication: March 2007
First Samhain Publishing, Ltd. print publication: September 2007

Dedication

To my wonderful husband John,
Who puts up with my constant scribbling with love and affection.

To my critique partner Nancy,
For her unfailing support and constant nagging.

To my sister Diana,
Who believed in my stories before I did.

To Sasha, Editor extraordinaire,
Who took a chance on a new writer.

Chapter One

The smile on Sara's face felt strained, her skin stretched tight over her high cheekbones, as she watched Cindy raise yet another toast to her. The irony that they were out celebrating her engagement and she was the one being the party pooper wasn't lost on her.

Cindy flipped her long wheat-colored hair over one shoulder and lifted her tequila into the air with unsteady hands. Liquor sloshed over the rim and spilled onto the laminated, faux-wood table between them. "To you and Mark, may you live happily ever after."

Sara set her drink down untouched. Cindy arched a perfectly sculpted blonde brow at her. "You know, I think it's bad luck not to drink when someone toasts you."

Elbows perched on the edge of the table, Sara bent forward and hollered over the loud thump of the bass ricocheting around them. "It might be bad luck, but if you insist that I drink one more shot of this sludge, I'm going to puke." Sara stuck out her tongue. "When I do, I'm going to aim for those new designer heels you're wearing."

Cindy blanched. "You wouldn't dare."

Sara hid an amused smile behind her hand. Cindy's strappy sandals probably cost more than her rent. "Bet me."

"All right, you win. No more alcohol tonight. I think I've had more than my fair share of tequila anyway."

"Yours and mine both, girl. You're going to have a hell of a hangover in the morning."

"Nope, you know I don't get hangovers. Besides, even if I did, it would be well worth it. How many times does a girl get to celebrate her best friend's engagement?"

Apparently twice, Sara thought with a touch of bitterness that came as no surprise. She slid her drink across the table to Cindy. "Here, you can have mine. Unlike you, my head will be pounding in the morning from the two I've already managed to gag down."

Cindy latched onto Sara's left hand before she could pull it back. She twisted the two-carat diamond engagement ring on Sara's finger, giving it a playful tug. "You know you're lucky. Mark loves you to pieces."

"And I love him." *I'm just not in love with him.*

"Come on, let's get out on the dance floor. We need to shake what our mama's gave us." Without waiting for a reply, Cindy jumped up, Sara's hand still in hers, and tugged Sara out of the booth.

It was in the middle of the second song that Sara saw him.

The man stood alone at the back of the room, his hip propped against the wall beneath the glowing red exit sign. His face partially hidden in shadow, Sara couldn't make out many of his features, but what little she could see stopped her in her tracks.

It couldn't be...

Sara started across the room, weaving between the mass of people shaking their stuff all around her. If she could just get close enough to see his face, she would know. Then maybe her heart would stop trying to beat out of her chest and she would be able to breathe again.

Vaguely, as if through a glass wall, she heard Cindy call her name from somewhere behind her. She ignored her friend and continued toward the mystery man, afraid he would disappear if she took the time to stop and explain. Cindy wouldn't believe her anyway. No one ever did. They just shook their heads at her and smiled sadly, placating her as if she'd lost her mind.

Sara was beginning to see their point.

By the time she pushed and shoved her way over the crowded dance floor, the man was gone. Her gaze darted frantically around the room, searching for him.

He must have gone outside.

She shoved through the back door, shivering when the brisk night air washed over her sweaty skin. Rubbing her hands briskly up and down her arms to ward off the chill, Sara's gaze ate up the dark alley outside the club.

A moist palm slapped down on her shoulder. She whipped around, expecting to find him behind her, staring at her with those fathomless, pale blue eyes she remembered so well. Instead, Cindy stood there, a scowl on her face and what looked like pity in her eyes. The pity stung.

Sara's nose began to burn, a telltale sign she was about to cry. She sucked in a deep breath and pushed back the tears building behind her eyes before they could rush to the surface and embarrass her even more. She felt like such a damn fool.

"Are you okay?"

Sara turned away, staring back out into the darkness. "Yeah, I'm good. I just needed to get some fresh air."

Cindy moved to stand beside her, her arms crossed over her chest. "You never could lie worth a damn."

Busted. "Kiss my ass, Cindy."

"I'll pass. Thanks anyway, but it would take me the rest of the night to cover every inch of that huge caboose you've got."

"Fuck you," Sara said with a laughing snort. "My ass is fine. Not all women want to be built like a stick figure, you scarecrow." It was the same inside joke they'd shared since ninth grade, when Cindy had sprouted up to just beneath six feet, her body long and lanky like a supermodel, while Sara forever remained short, and on the borderline between curvy and chubby.

"Want to tell me what had you running outside like the hounds of hell were nipping at your heels?"

"Nothing, I told you I just needed some air."

"Yeah right, and I'm the queen of England."

Sara gave a curt nod. "Your majesty."

"Smart-ass."

"Will you just let it go?"

"I don't know," Cindy replied quietly. "When will you?"

"What's that supposed to mean?"

"I think you know exactly what I mean, Sara. When are you going to let the man go? Tristan has been gone for six years. He's not coming back."

"You think I don't know that, damn it? You make it sound like he just left me. He didn't. He died." Her voice choked on the last words, preventing her from saying anything else. Knowing she was the object of her friend's pity was bad enough. She didn't want to make things any worse by crying.

"You've got to quit chasing his ghost, Sara. I thought when you finally accepted Mark's proposal that you were ready to move on."

"I am." When Cindy only continued to eye her in disbelief, Sara sighed loudly. "I'm trying to."

"Mm-hmm. Who are you trying to convince, you or me?"

"Can we just drop it?" *Please.*

"Yeah, for now, but you've got to let him go, girl. Mark doesn't deserve to play second fiddle to a dead man for the rest of his life. It's not fair to him."

Since when is life fair? Sara bit down on her bottom lip so hard she tasted the coppery tang of blood. It was the same lecture her friend had given her on more occasions than she cared to remember. Knowing Cindy was right didn't make it any easier to listen to.

Mark loved her. He was good to her and Sam. Hell, he'd asked her to marry him. Wanted to adopt her son. She should be down on her knees thanking God for him. Lord knew he'd long since proven himself to her, been the one anchor who kept her grounded through Tristan's disappearance. Mark had comforted her every night she'd cried herself to sleep, knowing the child she carried would never know his father. If there was any man alive she should be in love with, it was Mark.

Cindy pulled open the back door to the club. "Come on, Sara, let's go back inside and grab our coats. I think we've both had enough excitement for one night."

The back of Sara's neck prickled. She spun around, sure someone was staring at her. Her shoulders slumped when the alleyway appeared just as empty as it had the second before. Sara turned and followed Cindy back inside.

He stood in the shadows. His heart galloped against his rib cage while he watched the two women reenter the club.

Realizing how close he'd come to being discovered, his brow broke out in a nervous sweat. Tonight had been a close call. Too close. He needed to be much more careful in the future.

As it was, he'd barely been able to restrain himself. It took almost more willpower than he possessed to keep himself from going to Sara, wrapping her in his arms and promising her everything would be okay from now on. It was a lie, but he longed to say the words and mean them all the same.

Seeing Sara again, inside the smoky bar, had caught him off guard. He'd been so intent on his mission he hadn't even noticed Sara among the crowd until she was damn near on top of him.

His negligence was unacceptable. Not to mention dangerous in his line of work. Something he couldn't afford to let happen again.

Though unsure about what the specific repercussions were for an identified operative, he was smart enough to know it wouldn't be something as simple as a slap on the wrist. Chances were better than good that it would result in his death. A real one this time.

Tristan McKade was dead and buried. No matter how much he might wish otherwise, it had to stay that way.

Chapter Two

Lost in a maze of deep thought, Sara failed to notice the cab rolling to a stop in front of her house until Cindy spoke, startling her.

"Well, here you are, home, sweet home."

"Yeah." Sara looked out the window. "Listen, I'm sorry about tonight. Sorry I freaked out there at the end."

"It's okay, hun."

"No, I mean it. I think Mark finally popping the question has me a little shook up." Sara sighed, a long, drawn-out exhalation. "I've let Tristan go. I really have, but for some reason there's still this small part of me that feels guilty as hell about agreeing to marry Mark. I know it's stupid, but it feels like I'm being unfaithful."

"Tristan loved you. He would want you to be happy."

"I know. Sometimes I just wonder if he would want it to be with Mark."

"Mark was like a brother to him. I can't think of anyone else he would have chosen to be there for you and Sam."

The cabbie glared impatiently over his shoulder at them.

"Well…I guess I better get inside." Sara scrambled out onto the sidewalk. "Thanks for tonight. I'll return the favor when you get engaged."

Cindy snorted. "That will never happen."

"We'll see." Sara laughed. "Good night."

"Night. Give the little one a kiss for me."

"I will."

Sara closed the door and stood back on the curb, watching as the cab drove away. She used an extra few seconds to collect her thoughts before going into the house. Mark waited for her inside, having volunteered to stay with Sam so she could go out with Cindy. She didn't want him to see the inner turmoil she felt. The man had an uncanny ability to read her.

Having Mark in her life was such a blessing. Without him by her side she wouldn't have made it through the last six years. After Tristan was declared missing in action and presumed dead, she fell apart. Learning she was pregnant not long afterward hadn't made things any easier. Mark's friendship meant the world to her. He'd been like her very own guardian angel, swooping down to help her pick up the broken pieces of her life.

Her psychotic episodes hurt Mark, adding yet another layer to the guilt she carried. He couldn't understand her inability to let go of Tristan and move on with her life. Granted, she didn't have them as often as she used to. At first, she'd imagined Tristan on every street corner. Seen him everywhere she went. Gradually, with the help of a good therapist, she'd worked out most of her issues and began trying to put the past behind her. It hadn't been an easy road, but she'd thought she was doing better. Until tonight's episode, that is. It had been so long since the last one she'd deluded herself into thinking that part of her grief was behind her. That having Tristan appear as a figment of her imagination was a thing of the past.

Apparently not.

Lost in her musings, Sara startled when she noticed Mark standing in the open doorway, watching her with a curious smile on his handsome face. "Cinderella's home early. I didn't expect to see you before all the bars in the city closed."

Sara forced herself to smile. "What can I say? I missed my men."

Seeing him, she wondered again why she couldn't make herself fall in love with him. He was kind, loving and thoughtful, not to mention built like a God, tall and leanly muscled. His sandy blond hair and warm chocolate eyes gave him a boyish charm most women would adore. He was Mr. Perfect. It was too bad she couldn't transform herself into Mrs. Perfect.

Mark took her hand and helped her up the stairs. "Did you girls have fun tonight?"

"Yep. We had a blast. How did your evening go? Did Sam behave himself?"

"Of course he did. We had fun. Did lots of manly bonding rituals."

"Oh really? Like what, hunting and gossiping about women?"

"Nope. We colored and then he fell asleep on the sofa watching cartoons."

Thinking of her son brought a genuine smile to Sara's face. "It sounds like I missed out on a good time."

"Don't worry, now that you're home I'll make it up to you. We can have our own bonding session. I'm thinking maybe something a little more exciting than cartoons and crayon drawings though."

Mark held his arms out to her and Sara walked into his embrace, glad to be home. "What do you have in mind?"

He wrapped his arms around her and pulled her flush against his body. "Oh I don't know. I'm sure I can come up with something," he whispered against her neck, his firm lips trailing moist kisses over her skin.

Mark's penis swelled against Sara's stomach, the stiff outline poking into her abdomen. She leaned back, her hands on his shoulders, and stared up at him. "I like the way your mind works, Mr. Reynolds. Just hold that thought for a few minutes. I want to go up and look in on Sam."

"Okay. You go on ahead. I'll lock up down here."

"Thank you," she said.

"For what?"

"For watching Sam. For being you."

"You're welcome, and thank you."

"I hate to sound like a parrot but for what?"

Mark brushed his lips over hers. "For agreeing to be my wife."

"Oh, I think I got the best end of that deal." She stretched up on the tips of her toes and pressed her lips harder against his, grinding their mouths together before licking at the closed seam of his lips. "Are you staying tonight?"

"Wild horses couldn't drag me away." Mark swatted her on the bottom playfully. "Go on upstairs. I'll meet you up there."

Sara hurried up the stairs and crept quietly into her son's bedroom. She tiptoed through the maze of toys littering the floor to stand at his bedside and look down at her little boy's sweet face. Amazed as always by how perfect he was.

Sam appeared so peaceful when he slept. So at odds with what he was like while awake. Then he was a little devil, into everything he could get his hands on, and so full of life and energy. He asked questions nonstop, trying to learn everything about the world around him.

With a feather-light touch, she traced one baby-soft, chubby cheek. He was the one thing she'd done right in her life. Her best accomplishment. She was so very proud to be Sam's mom and she knew deep in her heart, where it counted, that Tristan would have been proud to be his dad.

Pressing a kiss on top of his head, Sara turned away and left before she started to feel even more maudlin than she already did.

She entered her room and mechanically undressed, crawling into bed and pulling the covers up to her chin. As an afterthought, Sara worked Mark's engagement ring off her finger and leaned over to set it in a ceramic dish on the nightstand. The ring was beautiful, the stone exquisitely cut and sparkly, but a bit too large for her, since she wasn't accustomed to wearing anything more than her mother's locket in the way of jewelry. The extra weight on her finger would take some time to get used to. Until then, it wasn't such a good idea to wear it to bed. Only the morning before, she'd tried to gouge her eye out with it upon waking and rubbing her face. Sara snuggled up under the blankets and waited for Mark to join her.

It was always the same routine. She would come upstairs and undress. Mark would give her a few minutes to herself and then join her. They would talk about their day, finally make love and go to sleep.

It would have been nice if just once they could skip all the pleasantries. If for once, Mark would quit being such a gentleman and just fuck her. Sara knew she could make a move on him at any time and he would respond, but it wouldn't have felt the same. She wanted him to be the one in charge, taking her, not the other way around. Being the dominant one in their sexual relationship didn't appeal to her. She wanted to be the one dominated. Making love had its time and place but sometimes Sara didn't want love and tenderness. She longed for him to take her, to be rough with her and make her enjoy it.

Fat chance of that happening.

A short moment later, Mark walked into the room. Sara sat up against the headboard, watching as he methodically stripped off his clothes. His white polo was the first thing to go. It came off over his head, revealing a broad chest and toned abdomen, lightly sprinkled with fine blond hair. His stomach muscles rippled pleasingly as he tugged the belt free of his pants. Left in only a pair of white cotton skivvies, he bent to retrieve and fold his clothing, neatly placing them on the dresser before sliding beneath the cool sheets.

Mark rolled onto his side and faced her, his elbow propped beneath his head. The blunt edge of his fingertips skimmed along the ridge of her collarbone. "Sam asked me if I was going to be his dad after we get married."

Sweet Jesus, her baby was growing up so fast. "What did you tell him?"

Mark's lips followed the path his fingers made along her skin. His hot breath wafted over the wet trail and her nipples began to stiffen, goose bumps rising on her flesh. "I said I would be his stepdad. Sam then asked if he could start calling me Dad instead of Uncle Mark."

"He did?" Her voice squeaked, causing her to wince. Mark lifted his head and looked down at her with heavy-lidded eyes. "Would that really be so bad, Sara? Sam needs a father."

"He has a father." As soon as the words left her mouth, she regretted them. *Open mouth, insert foot.*

Mark moved to the side of the bed, swung his legs over the edge and clicked on the bedside lamp. Harsh light flooded the mattress. "Do you love me?"

"Don't be silly. Of course I do. Otherwise, I wouldn't have agreed to be your wife."

"So let me see if I understand this. You love me. I'm good enough to be your husband, the father of any children we might have together, yet I'm not good enough to be a father to Sam."

When he put it that way she really felt like a bitch. "It's not like that."

Mark turned to her, his eyes shiny. "Then how is it, Sara? Explain it to me, because I'm having a really hard time trying to figure out what you want from me."

"I just want Sam to know who his real father is. I want him to know that he was wanted, even if Tristan never had the chance to know about him."

"I'm not trying to take Tristan's place in Sam's life. I love that boy like he was my own. Hell, Sara, I've been there for both of you since before he was born. I don't see the harm in letting him call me Dad if he wants to."

Why did this have to be so hard? Why couldn't she ever seem to please anyone enough?

Sara blew out a deep breath of hot air. "I suppose you're right. I'm just being touchy about it."

The happiness that suffused Mark's eyes made her feel guilty. She hadn't agreed to anything. Only sidestepped the issue for now.

Sara patted the bed beside her and let go of the sheet. It slid down her chest, pooling in her lap. She hoped the sight of her naked breasts would be too enticing for him to resist. "Come back over here, Mark."

There was one surefire method of shutting a man up and she wasn't above using it. Not tonight. She was so tired of all the talking and discussions...of everything. She didn't want to think about anything else tonight.

Relief coursed through her as he took the bait, flipping off the light and rolling toward her. His firm lips latched onto one of her nipples and began to suckle. The sharp edge of his teeth grazed over her skin, causing Sara to moan. "Don't stop."

Mark grunted in response, his mouth busy tending to more pleasurable pursuits. Lips, teeth and tongue worked on her breasts until her back bowed and her pussy wept. Undistinguishable noises flew from her mouth.

After what seemed an eternity, his mouth released her and he shifted to tower above her, his larger frame covering her like a human blanket. A condom appeared in his hand. He handed it to her and she unrolled it over him quickly, wanting him inside her, filling the emptiness that never seemed to go away anymore.

Then he was there, taking his place between her thighs. She wrapped her legs around him, her heels locking together in the small of his back. "Hurry, Mark. I need you—oh!" Her breath left her in a whoosh of hot air as he thrust inside her.

His lean hips retreated until only the flared head of his cock remained lodged within her. He slowly sank back inside, inch by excruciating inch. He repeated the torturous strokes over and over, again and again, until Sara thought she would die of want. She begged and pleaded, clawed and cursed. Still he persisted, keeping the pace and rhythm languorous.

The tension of imminent orgasm began to build in the pit of her stomach. It twisted and coiled, tighter and tighter until the world around her ceased to exist. All she knew was the feel of the hard cock pumping in and out of her clinging body and the orgasm breaking over her like ripples in a pond. Sara moaned, her wet sheath clenching around the hot invading length of his swollen penis.

Distantly, from deep inside her mind where her subconscious had retreated, she heard Mark groan her name as he reached his own release.

୧◯୨

Tristan McKade sighed in disgust as he pulled open the door to the dingy second-floor apartment he shared with his partner Shamus Long, better known to the few who knew of his existence as Shame.

Though Tristan had never been a man used to the finer things in life, he still would have been doing the cockroach-infested building a favor by classifying it as a shit-hole. Although the current living arrangements weren't the worst he'd ever been forced to endure, the assignment itself was.

He and Shame had been sent in, once again, to track down a madman. It was their job, along with the ten other specially recruited men currently on other various assignments, to hunt down rogue homeland terrorists and bring them to justice. At least that's what it said on paper.

Their true job was to police the unknown things that went bump in the night. The supernatural creatures that horror novelists only believed to exist within their warped imaginations.

He and Shame were both recruited six years earlier, straight from the army, after their Special Ops team was ambushed. A chill raced down his spine as he recalled the events leading up to his current lot in life.

Both he and Shame had been stationed on watch that night. Cold as hell outside, he remembered the way his breath puffed out in white, crystalline clouds of air. They kept warm by walking the rough terrain surrounding the base, patrolling.

Bored out of their minds, they'd crossed paths and stopped to shoot the shit when enemy fire broke out. A sharp biting sting punched him in the chest. Another in the groin. He hit the ground, knocking the air from his lungs, as gunfire and incomprehensible shouts echoed in his ears. And then nothing.

When he came to, he found himself in a sterile, white infirmary. A grizzly bear of an old man, dressed in a white lab coat and cotton scrubs, stood at his bedside. The man he would later call his boss calmly explained things to him. Crazy-sounding things that made Tristan think he'd lost his mind. Things only an insane man would believe.

The man towered over his hospital bed, looking down at him with strangely familiar, sympathetic eyes and introduced himself as John Ramsey. Said he was in charge of the ward Tristan had been placed in and then went on to explain that Tristan had been killed in the line of duty.

"Killed?" Tristan had said laughing. "How could I have been killed, if I'm still here talking to you, old man?"

The man just shook his head sadly as if he'd expected better of him. "Son, you were dead. No one could survive the number of bullets you were hit with." His cold hands pulled back Tristan's hospital gown and pointed out the bandage over his heart, a second one lower down, covering his groin. Tristan took one hard look at the thick white bandage over his cock and began to hyperventilate.

Ramsey patted him on the back, rubbing his paws over him in slow circles until his breathing evened out. "Now don't worry, all your parts are there. It may not be your original equipment but the organs we replaced them with are just as good." His silver eyes shot a glance at Tristan's groin. "Maybe better. Anyway, son, as I was saying...the only reason you're still breathing is because your dying body was sent here, to us, instead of home in a body bag. The scientists and I managed to do what only God above has been able to do before now. We decided to give you a second chance at life. A chance to make a difference in the world, if you accept our offer. It's fairly simple. You will leave your old life behind and work for us, in complete secrecy. Or we'll remove the *equipment* we replaced—your right lung, the right ventricle in your heart, your new tallywacker. And you'll get to meet your maker instead. The choice is yours."

Tristan couldn't contain the hysterical laughter that burst from his chest. "What the hell are you trying to pull on me?"

"This is no joke, son." Ramsey plucked a file off the tray stand next to Tristan's bed and held it out to him. "Classified" and the letters SCS were scrolled across the front in bold lettering. "You have a choice to make. Take your time, son, but make sure you think long and hard before you make your final decision because there's no going back once it's made." With that said, he strode from the room and slammed the heavy door shut behind him. The ominous sound of a deadbolt sliding into place echoed through the silent room.

And so Tristan's new life began. It wasn't until some long, lonely months later that he'd learned of Shame being tucked away inside the compound with him. They were the first of their kind, but not the last. A troop of genetically enhanced soldiers, created for the sole purpose of working for the SCS, or Supernatural Control Squad.

Tristan shoved his memories back into the vault he rarely let them escape from and entered his temporary home.

Shame sat on the ratty floral sofa, a longneck beer bottle curved in one hand, a trashy peroxide blonde beneath the other. Tristan flopped down in the chair off to the side and watched, amused, as the woman writhed and moaned beneath his friend's skillful touch.

No sooner than he'd settled down to watch the spectacle in front of him, the woman's back bowed and she let out a scorching wail of completion. Her eyelids lifted heavily, opening wide when she saw him sitting across the room.

Tristan's lips twisted into a wry grin. "Don't let me interrupt."

Shame's amused green gaze met his. "You know that having a voyeur in the room isn't going to stop me. I like an audience." Running his fingers through his coarse auburn hair, Shame turned back to his companion.

The woman struggled off Shame's lap and rose to her feet, her hands clumsily trying to straighten her skimpy, blue dress back into place. Shame leaned in closer and whispered something into her ear. She sighed, apparently reassured by whatever he'd said, and Shame patted her on the bottom, pointing down the hall toward his bedroom. Taking the hint, she hurried from the room, her heels clicking on the cracked linoleum.

Waiting until the woman was out of sight, Shame finally turned his attention to Tristan. He smiled. "You always did have the worst timing, my friend."

"You can pick things back up where you left off after we're finished. It's almost time for our update. You of all people should know better than to keep the boss waiting."

"Yeah, I do. I still remember what happened the last time I was late for one of his stupid videoconferences. I'll be damned if

I want to spend another month in isolation just for a little slap and tickle."

"Smart decision."

"Fuck you, buddy."

"Maybe later," Tristan replied with a wolfish grin. "I don't want a month in isolation either."

"Asshole."

Together they walked down the hall and entered the one room in the apartment that didn't look like it belonged in a crack house. The latest technological gadgets known to man were set up inside, most of them still years away from being released to the general public. The equipment gave them a much-needed edge over their quarries.

Shame fidgeted just inside the doorway. Tristan scowled at him as he sat in front of the computer. "I'll log in. You make sure your little friend is going to stay put while we get this over with. Make it quick though, I don't have all night."

Chapter Three

Tristan had just signed into the secure server when Shame waltzed back into the room. "We're almost in. Get over here behind me so the webcam can pick your ugly ass up on it."

"That's not what you were saying the other night."

"Whatever, now shut the hell up," Tristan replied shortly.

"Excuse me," a loud voice boomed out of the computer speakers.

Tristan jerked around and stared at the visage of his boss over the seventeen-inch monitor. "Sorry, sir, I wasn't speaking to you, sir." Shame snorted from behind him and Tristan wished he could elbow the bastard in the ribs. The little fuck was going to get them in trouble, again.

"No, I don't imagine you were. Now down to business. What new information do you have?"

"I'm sorry to say, not much, sir. I had no choice but to abort tonight's rendezvous before I could meet with the informant."

"Why is that? This mission should be your one and only concern."

"It is, sir. I assure you it is, but there were unforeseen complications."

"How so?" Ramsey's face began to turn a very unattractive shade of red. Of all the virtues their boss possessed, patience was not one of them. Tristan wondered what would happen if he told the old man that red really wasn't his best color.

"As I'm sure you know, sir, the city you currently have us stationed in happens to be my hometown. Tonight, while I was waiting at the location our informant designated, I noticed a woman who would've recognized me, had she been aware of my presence."

Although Tristan regretted the small lie to his boss, he felt it was justified. The man simply didn't need to know everything all the time. Especially that he was chased and damn near caught by the one person he'd been forbidden contact with.

"Rather than risk exposure, I left."

"Very well. Who was the person who may have seen you?"

"No one important, sir." *Please drop it.*

"Soldier, I insist you give me the name of the person you abandoned your post for."

"I'd rather not say, sir." Damn it, why couldn't the old man just let the matter drop? He didn't know why he expected any different. The bastard was relentless when it came to something he wanted.

"The name. Now. That's an order, soldier."

Shit.

"Sara. Sara McCoy."

Shame sucked in a deep breath behind Tristan. Ramsey's mouth stretched into a grim line, the corners turning white with tension.

Lowering his head, Tristan looked directly into the camera, pleading with his boss to read in his eyes what he dared not say with words. "She didn't see me, sir."

"Fine, soldier, we'll let the matter go, for now. We have more important matters at hand."

The rest of the transmission went smoothly. With a killer on the loose, there was little time to spare discussing other issues. For which Tristan was thankful. He knew the matter would be revisited as soon as their assignment concluded, but he would cross that bridge once he got there. While he could care less about what happened to him, he refused to let any harm come to Sara simply because she'd been in the wrong place at the right time.

As soon as the monitor went blank Shame pulled Tristan's chair around to face him. "Jesus. When were you going to tell me?"

He could see the concern for him etched into his partner's face. "It's not important. Let's just forget it happened."

"Don't bullshit a bullshitter. I know you, man. There's more to this than what you told the old man. Now out with it."

"It's not a big deal."

"It's not a big deal my ass, bro."

"Will you shut the hell up about it if I tell you?"

"Yeah."

"Okay, but you're going to be disappointed. Nothing happened. I was in the club, where we'd scheduled to meet the informant. I stood in the back, waiting for the SOB to show up and the next thing I know, Sara's headed right for me. I went out the back and hid until she left. It was all very manly. I felt like a damn pussy."

"I bet you did."

"Mmm-hmm," Tristan murmured.

"At least you got to see her, man. I would give my left nut to see my Maria one more time."

Tristan wasn't surprised Shame understood him so well. They were friends, team members, even before their change in circumstance. Since then, they'd been practically joined at the hip, partnered together on every assignment that came their way. While he wouldn't admit it out loud, it was comforting to have someone there who could understand him and know what he was going through.

It had been good to see Sara again. Too good.

The what ifs that plagued him constantly after he'd first started with the company were coming back to bite him in the ass now. Once again he found himself playing the old game in his head. What if none of this fucked-up shit had ever happened? What if he went to Sara and told her the truth about him? What if they both just disappeared one day? Would anyone bother to search for them? What if. What if. It was going to drive him out of his ever-loving mind.

Tristan patted Shame on the back. "I know you would, man." Unlike Tristan, who'd only lost the woman he loved, Shame had lost a wife and a daughter. Though he couldn't contact them, Shame kept discreet tabs on them through channels Tristan felt better not knowing anything about. The less he knew, the less he could be forced to tell under interrogation.

Shame offered to look in on Sara for him a few times over the years, but Tristan declined. While he prayed she was happy, he didn't want to know the details. It was selfish, he knew, but he didn't think he'd survive hearing about how she'd moved on without him. That she was married to some other man, having that man's children instead of his.

"Listen, dude, it's been a long-ass day. My entertainment for the night is waiting on me."

"Go on then, you don't need to baby-sit me."

"No, I don't. I thought you might like to join us though. Have a little fun for a change."

"No. You know I'm not..."

A roguish smile spread across Shame's face. "Yeah. Yeah. I know you don't fuck women anymore. I'll do her. You can do me."

Tristan laughed at his friend's bawdy comment. Shame's idea wasn't such a bad one. If Tristan didn't find something to occupy his time, he would spend the rest of the night awake, thinking forbidden thoughts. Thoughts about Sara. "Sure. Why the hell not."

"Good." Shame slapped him on the back. "Go grab us a couple of beers out of the fridge, will you?"

"Yeah. You go on up and do your thing. I'll be there in a few."

Shame strode down the hall. He stopped at his bedroom door, his hand on the knob, and looked back at Tristan over his shoulder. "You're coming, right?"

Tristan smirked. "Hopefully not too fast." He tried to joke about the whole situation as if it were no big thing. When Shame didn't respond, only stared back at him, his deep green eyes reading more into the situation than Tristan wanted him to, Tristan dropped the act. "I said I would, didn't I?"

Shame nodded and entered his bedroom without another word, leaving the door ajar behind him.

Half an hour later, Tristan leaned against the wall, near the foot of Shame's bed. Dressed solely in a pair of unbuttoned jeans, Tristan focused his attention on the couple writhing atop the bed. The blonde lay supine, her arms restrained to the headboard with handcuffs. Her eyes squeezed shut, the woman's head flailed from side to side in passion. Pitiful wailing moans of ecstasy spilled from her mouth.

His partner's head was buried between her thighs, his tongue immersed in the wet folds of her sex, ravenously devouring every drop of cream his attentions brought forth.

To say Tristan was turned-on would have been an understatement. With each breath, the heady smell of aroused bodies and clean sweat, of sex incarnate cloyed the air around them. Young and healthy, his body responded as nature intended, his cock rising proud and stubborn against the inside of his pants.

Absentmindedly, Tristan kneaded his crotch, his fingers smoothing over the rigid outline of his cock, trying to appease the beast inside.

Not for the first time that night, Tristan wished he wasn't there. While his body craved sexual gratification, his heart lay cold and dead in his chest.

That didn't mean he was going to walk away from what Shame offered. Though raw sex was hardly succor for his soul, it was steps above his own clammy hand and the painfully cherished memories he harbored of being with Sara.

Shame's low moan of pleasure added to the slurping sounds already coming from between the blonde's firm thighs. Tristan's cock twitched within its denim prison, demanding its share of attention. Tristan pushed his thoughts away, shucked his jeans and approached the bed.

In his fist, he held the stalk of his thick and ruddy cock, slowly stroking up and down along its full length. With his other hand, he reached out to gently cup and palm the delicate orbs of Shame's sex, before gliding his fist up and over the rigid shaft above, gripping his friend's swollen erection much the same as he did his own.

Shame growled in response, his ass lifting higher, as his tongue burrowed deeper into the woman's pussy.

Closer to the action, Tristan was better able to see the intimate torture being inflicted on the woman's tender flesh. Two thick fingers ruthlessly shoved in and out of her pussy in time to the rhythm set above by Shame's flexible tongue lashing up and down over her clit.

Her body began to tremble and a shrill cry spilled from her puffy red lips, release sweeping over her. Before the last shudder faded, Shame was up and moving into position over her. He lined the swollen crown of his dick up with her cunt and rammed home in one long, furious thrust. Buried to the balls in hot, wet pussy, Shame froze and waited for Tristan to join them.

Lube in hand, Tristan climbed onto the bed. He poured a generous amount of the slick fluid into his palm and smoothed it over his own flushed erection. Taking a brief moment to enjoy the cool, slick glide of moisture over hot flesh, Tristan focused his attention on preparing Shame, slathering the valley between his friends steely buttocks with liquid. When Shame's ass glistened, Tristan stopped and fisted his cock, rubbing the flared head back and forth over the wet, wrinkled pucker of Shame's ass. His balls pulling up tight and needy against his groin, Tristan applied pressure and slowly began to guide himself inside, watching Shame's hole swallow his cock.

Shame cried out at the invasion and ground himself into the woman beneath him, even as Tristan forged onward, forcing the remaining inches of his cock deeper into the gripping depths of his partner's ass. Only stopping when he felt the wet smack of their balls slapping against each other. There Tristan stilled, sweat beading on his brow, and allowed Shame a chance to adjust to his larger-than-average size and girth.

Taking a deep breath, Tristan steadied himself and began to shuttle in and out of Shame in short, digging thrusts. He pulled his hips back, until only his crown was caught on the tight ring of muscle guarding Shame's entrance. Shame followed suit, withdrawing almost completely from the woman's pussy. Together they plunged forcefully back into the receptive flesh awaiting them; Tristan into Shame and Shame into the woman beneath him.

Tristan pumped harder and faster, trying to keep up with the furious rhythm Shame set. Sweat rolled down his torso and stung his eyes as he strained toward completion. A feminine shriek filled the room seconds before Shame's body locked up beneath his. Tristan shoved deep and froze, grunting as the silken walls around his cock clenched and sucked the climax from his body. Scalding ropes of semen shot from his dick and filled Shame's gripping channel as Tristan came, long and hard. When the aftershocks began to fade, Tristan retreated, carefully withdrawing his penis from its temporary haven.

Shame immediately fell onto his back and flung an arm over his face. The woman snuggled up to his side, apparently well sated and on her way to dreamland.

Tristan gathered up his clothes and quietly left the room.

Chapter Four

Two pots of coffee and six ibuprofen since waking up, and Sara still felt like a zombie with a hangover. She swore and bargained with any higher power listening that if they would just make her headache go away, she'd never drink again.

Her head only throbbed harder.

Her day started off crappy. As soon as her eyes opened she and Mark began to argue about the "daddy" saga that never seemed to end. Mark had even called her an unreasonable bitch. Maybe she was, but something about her son calling someone other than his biological father dad just didn't sit right with her.

Mark stormed out of the house in a huff, slamming the door behind him. Sam woke in a foul mood. Traffic had been hell, making her late for work. Again. She was pretty sure her day couldn't get any worse.

And then, the very last person she felt like having a confrontation with stormed toward her, a frown between his beady brown eyes. Lester Morgan, her sleazy boss at The Daily Tribune, was about as much fun to talk to as the wall.

From the moment she'd been hired as a receptionist ten months earlier, Morgan had harassed her about going out on a date with him. She'd thought he would eventually give up and move on to greener pastures, but not him. Either he didn't know the meaning of the word no or he thought she was playing hard to get.

Sara wasn't a mind reader, but it didn't take a genius to figure out what she could expect from him today. This morning had been her third strike. The third time she'd been late this month. According to company policy, that meant she would be placed on probation for the next ninety days. If she was late again, she would be waiting in the unemployment line.

Maybe a little sucking up was in order. Her lips curved into what she hoped looked like a sincere smile. "Good morning, Mr. Morgan. How are you today?"

"I've been better," he all but growled at her. "I'd like to have a word with you in my office, Ms. McCoy."

Before she could respond, he pivoted on his heels and stalked away, automatically assuming she would obediently follow along behind him like some brainless drone.

For a second, Sara was tempted to stay right where she was and see what his reaction would be when he turned around and figured out she wasn't behind him. She imagined his face going bright red and his head swelling up to impossible proportions right before it exploded, like in a morbid cartoon.

She stood still for a moment, calculating the amount left in her savings. *Not enough.*

Sara stifled her giggles and hurried to catch up with him.

Morgan closed the door and told her to have a seat. Never a good sign. He moved behind his desk, sat and picked up a ballpoint pen as she settled into the chair across from him. Annoyingly tapping the pen against the oak surface of his desk, Morgan glared at her.

The cold way he regarded her gave Sara the creeps. She felt like a naughty schoolgirl sent to the principal's office for misbehaving. She resisted the urge to tell him to get on with the lecture so she could go back to work, choosing to remain quiet instead.

"Do you know why I asked to speak with you this morning?"

"Yes. I think I do."

"Well what do you have to say in your defense?" His tapping picked up in tempo.

She lifted her chin. "I apologize for being late this morning. It won't happen again." *Until the next time.*

"I wasn't speaking of your repeated tardiness, Ms. McCoy." The incessant tapping stopped while he brushed his fingers through his thinning hair and continued to stare at her with an intense perusal that made her skin crawl.

"I'm not sure what you're talking about then, Mr. Morgan."

"Were you not at Club Metropolis last night?"

"Yes, I was. However, I fail to see what my personal life has to do with my job performance." Her hands gripped the arms of the chair. Were men only put on Earth for the sole purpose of torturing women?

If this was another attempt on his part to try to get her to go out with him, she was going to scream. Better yet, she could just tell him where he could stick his crappy job, once and for all. She'd rather take a job shoveling shit than put up with any more of his sexual harassment.

Hang on a second. How did he know where she'd been?

"If you don't understand what I'm talking about then you clearly don't read our paper." He started back up with the tapping, hitting the end of the pen harder against the desk. Each time it hit the glossy surface it made a loud ping that grated on her nerves.

What in the world was he getting at? "Of course I read our paper. I'm afraid I didn't have the pleasure this morning, because I overslept, but I normally read it every day." Sara frowned. "I'm still not sure exactly what it is you're driving at here, Mr. Morgan." She'd never read the paper in her life. She had no intention of trying to. Between dealing with her son and getting herself ready each morning, who had the extra time? Besides, it wasn't like she worked for a real newspaper. The Daily Tribune was a gossip rag. She had enough drama in her life, without having to read about other people's bologna.

"If you'd taken the time to read the paper this morning," he sighed, "then you would know what I'm referring to, wouldn't you?" His eyes narrowed. "Since you didn't, I'll have to tell you. The latest victim of The Mangler was discovered outside of Club Metropolis last night."

Sara knew he was still talking, she could see his mouth forming the words, but she couldn't make out a single syllable of what he said. She was too busy reeling from the news he'd just imparted. Another person had been murdered. How many did that make in the last six months? Five? Six? How many more poor women would have to be killed before the police caught the lunatic responsible?

A chill raced down her spine as something else occurred to her. He said the body had been found outside the club. The very same club where she'd been the night before. She'd chased a man, a very large man, into the alley behind the club. Was he the killer? Had she led him straight to his next victim?

Morgan cleared his throat. "Well?"

Sara looked back at her boss. "I'm sorry. What were you saying?"

His lips thinned, turning white around the edges. He wasn't a man who liked to repeat himself. "I said, I'd like to know why you didn't feel it necessary to make yourself available for an interview with one of our reporters. As I'm sure you know, our paper has been a key player in alerting the public about The Mangler's latest exploits. An interview with a possible witness would have a dramatic effect on our sales." With what looked like an afterthought he added, "And it would keep the people informed."

She bit down on her tongue—hard—to keep herself from asking how he could be such a coldhearted bastard. Some poor soul was murdered and all he wanted to talk about was newspaper sales. "I'm sorry. I wasn't aware there had been another murder last night. I most certainly didn't see anything that would be of interest to this newspaper or the general public. Rest assured that if I had, I would've gone to the proper officials right away.

"Is that all for now, Mr. Morgan? I really do need to get back to work." *And away from you, before I tell you what a sniveling little weenie you are.*

"Not yet. There is still the matter of your tardiness."

Damn, she'd forgotten all about that. "As I said, it won't be a problem in the future."

"You know, Sara, I would be willing to overlook this whole matter if you would agree to go out on a date with me. Say Friday night?"

Sara wanted to tell him that hell would freeze over first. Instead she smiled brightly and tried to damp down her gag reflex as lust briefly flickered over his rodent-like features. The bastard had some nerve.

"I'm very flattered, Mr. Morgan, but I'm afraid I'm already spoken for. In fact, last night's outing was an engagement celebration." She held her breath, waiting to see how the man would take another rejection from her. She disliked him and the job, but that didn't mean she needed it any less.

Morgan's nostrils flared. His gaze bore into her, combing over her face for who knew what. When he appeared satisfied with whatever he saw, he let out a deep breath and stood. "My congratulations on your engagement. Now if you'll excuse me, I do have a paper to run."

"Of course," she replied, sailing out the door before he changed his mind.

ಙಐ

The body of a young woman between the age of twenty and twenty-five had been found in the alley behind Club Metropolis. As with the other victims, she'd been raped and drained of all her blood, left out in the open for someone to find.

The perp seemed to get off on taunting them. Though he was careful not to leave behind evidence of what he was, the suspected vampire had a calling card that was unmistakable. The throat of each woman was ripped out, the jugular vein torn and ragged, unlike the straight edge a knife wound would leave behind. There was always the possibility that the perp was a Were, but it was slim. Wolves were known to devour their prey, or at the very least tear large chunks of flesh from the victim. These murders bore no such evidence.

The fact that he'd gotten away with it again was Tristan's fault. If he had been doing his job, instead of playing hide-and-seek with Sara, the woman would still be alive. Instead she lay lifeless on a cold slab in the city morgue. That he could have—should have—been there to prevent her death and hadn't, burned at his soul like toxic waste.

With few leads to go on, he and Shame decided to split up. Shame stayed behind, doing research, seeing what kind of new information he could gather from the crime scene evidence. Tristan went out and did what he did best—the footwork.

Their most promising lead at the moment was on a man named Lester Morgan, who owned a local gossip paper. It seemed that whenever a new body was found, his reporters were on the beat before any of the other journalists knew what was going on. In one instance, the first murder, one of Morgan's staff had even discovered the body and called in the police themselves.

It seemed like a piss-poor lead to Tristan but he knew better than to not scour all paths provided. It was entirely possibly that a wild-goose chase would lead him right where he needed to be. So, he sat outside the office of The Daily Tribune in a late-model green sedan with tinted windows and cased the joint. The building itself wasn't anything special, just brick and mortar. What he wanted to see, were the people who worked there. While Shame swore by lab work and forensics, Tristan was old-fashioned. He wanted to see the employees and the owner with his own two eyes, try to get a feel for them. His gut feelings were seldom wrong and he made it a point to listen to them. Doing so had saved his ass on more than one occasion.

At five o'clock on the dot, people started to file out the front exit. No one looked out of the ordinary. Tristan was planning his next step, possibly breaking into the office, when he saw Sara exit the building.

She wore an apricot skirt suit, her dark red hair pulled back at the nape of her neck in a messy bun. His breath caught as she looked right at him, like she knew he was there, watching her, before she turned and headed straight for a beat-up old Volvo.

Though he wanted to know why she'd been in the building, he had to put his curiosity on hold. He needed to stay and check out the inner office. Maybe even follow Morgan for a little while and see if he was up to anything fishy. Tristan didn't have time to mess around with anything else.

Fuck it.

He put the car in first gear and pulled out into traffic.

Tristan followed at a measured distance, careful not to be seen, as Sara drove out of town limits and stopped in front of a rickety old white house. Though it had seen better days, the house looked warm and inviting. A red and white swing set sat off to one side of the fenced-in yard. The rest of the lawn was littered with various children's toys.

He wondered if she lived there, if the contents of the yard belonged to her children. Circling around the block, Tristan chose a driveway a couple of houses down and parked, waiting to see what would happen next. Whether she would knock or go straight in.

Tristan breathed a sigh of relief when Sara knocked on the front door. It wasn't her house. A rotund woman with steel-wool-colored hair came to the door, a welcoming smile on her round face, and let Sara in.

Who was the woman? Tristan knew she wasn't a relative. Like him, Sara was an orphan. Her mother committed suicide when Sara was five, leaving her to be raised in foster care.

Sara had only been inside a few minutes when she came out. She calmly walked down the sidewalk, toward her car. She wasn't who caught his attention though. A little boy clutched Sara's hand. Tristan couldn't tear his gaze away from the child. His entire world came to a crashing halt. He couldn't move. He couldn't fill his lungs.

He had a son.

The boy was the spitting image of Tristan when he was a child. They shared the same black hair and bone structure. There was no way the kid could belong to anyone else. He had a son. All these years and he'd never known, never even suspected.

Motionless, he sat and watched as Sara helped his son into the car and drove away. He didn't move, just stared at the empty space where the car once sat.

Some time later, Tristan snapped out of his daze. *Holy shit*, he was a father. With a renewed purpose in life, he backed out of the driveway and sped off into the night. He didn't know how to find Sara, but he knew someone who did.

It was time to take Shame up on his offer.

Chapter Five

Sara spent all day Saturday shopping with Cindy. By the time she insisted they call it a day, her eyes were blurry from all the different shades of white dresses they'd ohhed and ahhed over, and she was ready to collapse from exhaustion. She really hated to shop. It was so much easier to order things online, but picking out her wedding dress via the Internet didn't seem like such a good idea. Skipping the hoopla and eloping began to sound better by the minute. Or better yet, they could forget about the whole thing and live together. Mark was practically living in her house as it was. They could just make it permanent. Sara tried to think of a good way to broach the subject with Mark as she drove Cindy home.

Reversing out of Cindy's driveway, the hair on the back of her neck stood up and her skin began to tingle. Someone was staring at her. She hit the brakes and whipped around in her seat, trying to see who it was. Not a single soul was anywhere to be found.

You're losing it, girl.

Sara snorted. Weird stuff had been happening to her all week. She had spotted the Tristan look-alike at the club, and then she could have sworn she was being followed by the same car all week. Everywhere she went...there it was. She'd even pointed it out to Mark when they'd shopped for groceries. He'd looked at her like she was missing a few screws upstairs and patiently explained, in his calm manner, that there were probably a thousand vehicles that all looked like that on the road in their area. What she considered to be one car was more than likely several different ones of the same make and model.

Sara laughed it off and chalked the whole thing up to paranoia, but the truth was she didn't feel like she'd only imagined it. Ever since her impromptu talk with her boss earlier in the week, she'd felt as if someone was out there, watching her.

She knew her fears were unfounded, that no one was out to get her, but no matter how hard she tried, she couldn't get rid of the odd sense of foreboding surrounding everything she did. Thankfully, it had been a busy week. There hadn't been any time to dwell on much of anything other than work and the usual mundane day-to-day activities of life.

Sara pulled up to her house and opened the car door. She slid out and slammed it behind her. She was reaching through the open back window to grab her things, when something large and furry barreled into her, tackling her to the ground.

"Mom! Look what Uncle Mark got me!" Sam bounced across the lawn, full of energy and excitement, pointing at the large dog lying on top of her. "Isn't he great? I named him Bob. We can keep him, right? Uncle Mark said we could." His big baby blues gazed adoringly down at her. How would she ever be able to say no to that face?

Sara climbed to her feet and pulled her wiggling son into her arms, kissing him soundly on the cheek. "Sure we can, honey. He's a great dog."

She shot daggers at Mark as he trotted down the porch steps. She hoped he realized how much trouble he was in. What was she supposed to do with a dog?

"Mark, can I have a word with you in the kitchen?"

"Uh, sure." He turned to follow her in, hollering at Sam over his shoulder. "Make sure you stay in the yard, Sam. Your mom and I will be right back." Sam ignored him and continued to roll around on the grass with his new best friend.

Sara lashed out at him as soon as the door shut behind them. "How could you get a dog? I barely have enough time and energy to take care of myself and Sam as it is without having to worry about housebreaking a dog!"

"He's just a puppy. He won't be that much extra work. Besides, Sam can take care of him. It will teach him some responsibility." He smiled at her, the dimples in his cheeks popping out.

The dog had to go. That sexy smile of Mark's was not going to make her melt. *It wasn't.* "If you really believe that a five-year-old is capable of taking care of a dog then you're delusional. This is the last thing I need to deal with right now."

"Sara, honey, it will be okay. Sam can walk him in the yard and feed him. All you will have to do is help me housebreak him. Okay? I promise I'll be here to help pick up the slack more from now on." He tugged her up against him, her back to his chest, as they stood staring out the window at her son. "You can't stay mad at me about this. Look how happy he is."

Damn, the man played dirty.

Sara gave in, letting herself snuggle into the crook of his arm. She stood with him, watching Sam play with his new pet. He did look happy. Mark kissed her hair and pulled her a little closer. She could've stayed in that moment forever, with Mark's arms around her and her son running around happily playing in the yard.

"All right, you win. The dog can stay, but you have to help me with him. I just wish you'd talked to me about it first." Sara tilted her head back and enjoyed the feel of Mark's soft lips sliding over hers.

ಬಿಂ

Exhausted from another long night of trailing Lester Morgan and following him through the mundane activities of having dinner and shopping for God knows what at the twenty-plus stores he'd frequented that night, Tristan had come to the conclusion that Morgan was not their man. He was a night owl, but the man couldn't be who they were looking for, nobody that damn boring could be their killer.

Shame had had little to no luck with the minute amount of evidence he'd been able to collect from the old crime scenes and they were still waiting on the higher-ups to cut through all the bureaucratic red tape in order to grant them access to what the police had in storage. Shame wasn't willing to commit a guess about Morgan's innocence or guilt, but he did agree with Tristan regarding their perp being a thrill seeker. Morgan simply didn't fit that profile and there was exactly zero evidence that he was anything other than a normal, if dull, human.

Tristan had crossed him off his possible list of suspects and decided to take another look at the man's employees. He wasn't sure how, but that newspaper was somehow connected to the deaths. He was sure of it.

Now, finally home at half past one a.m., Tristan rested his back against the wall, his long legs comfortably stretched out over the length of his California king bed. In his hands he held the background report Shame had procured for him earlier in the week. The fragile sheets of printer paper had already begun to crinkle and wear thin around the edges from repeated handling.

Sara's entire story lay before him, the bare bones of her life printed out in ink. Most of it he already knew, or had been a part of. Only the last few pages held new information. Those were the sheets he held. Everything he wanted to know was right there, all the information he'd asked Shame to ferret out against his own better judgment.

He read through it all again now, although he didn't need to. Thanks to the technology pumped into him years before, he possessed a photographic memory and could visualize the sheets of paper in his mind without actually looking at them. Yet he still did. Somehow holding the pages made him feel a measure closer to Sara and their son. Like holding something so inconsequential could make him a part of their lives.

And the child was his son. Of that there had been no doubt of from the moment he had laid eyes on him. Shame had found a copy of the child's birth record and included it along with the other information. He ran his fingers along the printed name on the birth certificate, Samuel Tristan McCoy. That was his five-year-old son's name.

His thoughts had been in constant turmoil since he'd seen his name there, listed as the boy's father. Two tiny words kept running through his head, over and over, and fucking with his concentration. *His son.* He couldn't think of anything else.

He and Sara's love for one another had created a life.

Tristan's heart beat faster, overcome by emotion. He figured Samuel must've been conceived on his last leave. He'd only been home a week, seven short days and nights to spend with the woman he loved. Every minute of it was spent alone, he and Sara together, making love and planning their future. Dreaming of what their life would be like when he was discharged from service in six months. When they would be able to afford to get married and buy a quaint little starter house, build a family of their own. A family they both wanted, since neither of them had had one.

Accepting the way things were in his life now was hard enough without the added complication of a child being involved. It was damn near impossible for him to keep his distance from Sara, but he'd managed. The knowledge that Sara had borne him a son, one his superiors would expect him to forget as quickly as he had learned of him, slowly ripped what was left of his soul to shreds.

What surprised him was that he still had a soul left to be taken away. If someone had asked a week earlier, he would have denied having one. Would've said that he lived for his job, nothing more, nothing less. That was the way it had to be, his superiors wouldn't allow anything else.

Tristan kept a tight leash on his feelings, careful not to let the personal baggage he dragged around behind him, like a ball and chain, run over into his work. Well, he certainly wasn't in control now. The chip he carried on his shoulder was. He couldn't think. He couldn't focus.

In his line of work, that was as good as a death sentence. Losing your focus was not an option. It was stupid and dangerous. Not something he could afford to let happen.

His palms slapped down on the bed on either side of his hips. He needed to clear his head. Let old ghosts go and get back to work. There was only one thing he could do to make that happen. He needed to say goodbye.

෴

Sara woke in the middle of the night, her heart pounding and a thin sheen of sweat covering her body. Another nightmare. She'd been having the same dream for weeks.

Tugging off the covers, Sara shoved them over onto Mark. He grunted in his sleep and flung away the extra warmth, rolling further onto his side of the bed.

Sara headed into the bathroom and flipped on the light, quietly pulling the door closed behind her. She splashed some cool water on her face and stared into the mirror. She looked like shit. Her eyes were bloodshot, ringed by puffy blue crescents. Red curls stood out in every direction.

Definitely not going to win any beauty pageants.

Yawning, Sara ran a hand through her tangled hair. She wanted to crawl back under the covers next to Mark and get some sleep. From her appearance, she could definitely make use of the extra beauty rest.

Hell, who was she kidding? There was no way she would be able to go back to sleep tonight. Not while remnants of her nightmare still ran around in her head. What she could remember of it was the same as every other night.

Sara was alone in the dark. Unable to see around her. All she could make out was a light shining in an open doorway at the end of a very long hallway.

Someone screamed behind her, the bloodcurdling sound of it ricocheting through the inky darkness. Scared, Sara headed for the light, hands stretched out in front of her. Not matter how far she walked the light grew smaller and smaller, moving farther away.

That was when the screams would start again. She would take off at a run toward the little light which had become a beacon of hope, of safety. Just as she was close to reaching it, a hateful laugh would echo through the hall and the door would slam shut in her face, pitching her into complete darkness.

Then, always at that same point in the dream, she would wake up. Nothing about it ever changed.

Maybe she had watched one too many horror movies.

Sara longingly looked through the doorway at the bed. Nope, there would be no more sleeping for her tonight.

But there were several loads of laundry waiting for her downstairs in the basement. She might as well get something done while she was up.

Chapter Six

Tristan stood gazing down at his son. The boy was sound asleep in a blue racecar bed. Moonlight filtered in through the window above his bed, creating a gauzy halo around him.

Samuel was beautiful. Shaggy, mussed black hair framed the oval of his small face. Thick lashes rested against chubby cheeks that billowed out with each deep, slumbering breath he took. A small, red, bow-shaped mouth stood out in stark relief against his pale complexion. Tiny brown freckles dotted his nose.

He had his mother's skin tone, her mouth. The rest was pure daddy. Tristan's chest filled with pride. The love he and Sara shared had created this perfect little boy. Samuel.

Mine.

Tristan's fingers itched to reach out and touch him, to make sure he was real and not a figment of his imagination. He resisted. It was stupid of him to be there to begin with. He couldn't afford to take a chance on waking the cute tyke up. It was idiotic to even think about it.

Trained to make himself invisible, Tristan could move in and out of any building he wanted with no one the wiser. Tonight, stealing into Sara's house, he'd taken extra precautions not to alert anyone of his presence. He couldn't do anything foolish to mess that up. He'd put himself at risk enough just by coming here to say goodbye.

With reluctance, Tristan exited the room.

Stopping in the hallway, he shot a covetous glance at Sara's bedroom door, conflicted with emotions. The voice in his head told him to enter the room, take one last look at her before he fled. The better, wiser, part of him urged him not to, just to leave. She wasn't his anymore. Her heart belonged to Mark.

The bastard.

Something inside Tristan clenched painfully when he thought of Sara sharing her bed, her body with someone else. Even Mark. Especially Mark. At one time, the man had been like a brother to him. How he could so easily move in on Tristan's family bothered him more than if she'd been with a stranger.

He pushed the thought away before the urge to grab both Sara and Sam and run as far and fast as he could became too strong to resist. Taking one last look at her closed door, he turned his back to it and left the house as silently as he'd entered.

୨୦୧୫

Sara looked up from the dryer to see Bob, the dog, cocking his leg over her new self-propelled lawn mower.

"Shoo," she yelled, waving her arms at him. He looked up at her with big chocolate brown eyes and blinked.

Like she was the one being unreasonable.

She knew she was going to regret agreeing to keep the dang dog. Now her rash decision was coming back to bite her in the butt.

Sara ran up the basement steps and grabbed the dog's leash off the kitchen counter. There was no time like the present to teach Bob his place. She didn't want him to start thinking it was okay to use her house as his personal toilet.

She clipped the shiny new red leash on his matching collar and tugged. Bob didn't budge an inch. He sat back on his hind legs and licked his chops. The thought of using the bathroom outside didn't appear to be any more appealing to him than it would be for her.

Well, that was just too bad.

"Come on, Bob. Cooperate with me here." She yanked the leash again, putting more of her weight into the effort. This time he hopped up and followed at his own stubborn pace behind her. Thirty minutes later, Sara was still waiting for him to do his business. She'd led him around the backyard a dozen times, watching as he stopped to sniff random spots. It was dark. She was cold. And her patience was wearing thin. She was tempted to take him back in the house and say the hell with it. Mark could clean up the mess he made in the morning. That would serve him right. He was the one who bought the damn dog.

Sara pulled on Bob's leash. He growled at her.

Okay, he really wasn't ready to go back in yet.

"Come on, boy. Let's go back inside. If you had to do anything, you should've done it by now." The hackles on his back stood up. He crouched closer to the ground and growled louder, showing his teeth.

"What's wrong with you?" He couldn't be scared of her...could he? She reached down to smooth his fur, hoping to soothe him. He snarled and snapped at her, forcing Sara to jerk her hand back. *What the hell?* Was it possible for a dog to have multiple personalities?

Now what? It wasn't like she had any experience with animals. Other than the occasional fish, she'd never had a pet growing up. How were you supposed to calm down an irate dog? All she could think of was petting him. Since she didn't want to lose a finger, that wasn't a viable option. Maybe talking to him would help.

"Calm down, boy. It's okay. Everything's going to be just fine. Nobody is going to hurt you." Sara fidgeted. Talking to him wasn't cutting it. Bob still looked ready to attack. Should she stand still and hope he calmed down on his own, or run? Wouldn't dogs chase people if they ran? Dumb question. Of course they would. Damned if you do, damned if you don't, was starting to sound like her personal mantra.

Before she could make up her mind about what to do, Bob's growl intensified and he lunged...right at her. She spun around, ready to sprint back to the house, and ran face first into a man standing directly behind her.

Mark. Thank you, God.

She pursed her lips and looked up, ready to gush her thanks all over him. The man wasn't Mark. Her second thought...he wasn't a man.

Sara started to back up, her gaze locked on the person before her. The deformed bone structure, dead black eyes, pig snout and blood red lips looked like a child's Halloween mask but obviously wasn't. His thin lips receded, moving into a gross interpretation of a snarl. Sara gasped in horror as she caught sight of its teeth. Rows upon rows of sharp, pointy, serrated teeth filled the impossibly large cavern of his mouth, reminding her of a shark.

One of his hands shot out and wrapped around her arm, his fingers biting into her skin. "You're mine at last, sweet Sara."

"What the hell are you doing? Let go of me!" Sara fought against the man...thing. She trembled as his hold on her tightened to the point of pain. Who the hell was this freak? And how did he know her name?

Sara fought harder, her free hand beating at his chest, slippered feet kicking out at him. She even tried to headbutt him, all to no effect. He responded to her struggles with a dark laugh, evil in its sinister glee. "Are you going to calm down now?" When she didn't answer, only continued to hit and kick, he raised her off the ground and shook her as if she weighed no more than a child's plaything. "You will calm down." His voice grew louder and deeper. "Right now."

Sara's mind locked up. Her fists beat weakly against the beast's immovable chest. Her body fought against her entrapment, but she couldn't tear her gaze away from its hideous face. It was like looking at a car wreck, it was bad, you knew better than to stare, but you couldn't help yourself.

The corners of her vision began to blur and turn black. *No!* She would not pass out. Sara willed herself to stay alert, to keep fighting even though she knew he was too strong for her. If she was going to die, she wouldn't make it easy for him. She was damn sure going to make the bastard fight for his supper.

Sara broke through her body's paralysis and attacked. She did the only thing she hadn't tried up till that point. She kneed him in the balls. He howled in pain and released her, his hands flying to his groin to rub at himself. She spun around and ran, scrambling to get away before he recovered enough to come after her.

"You're going to pay for that, bitch."

Sara wanted to look behind her but didn't. He sounded much too close for her peace of mind. She willed her legs to move faster.

Cruel hands latched onto her hair and yanked her backward. Her scalp screamed in pain, her eyes filling with moisture. She balled a fist and swung it around at the thing's head. He caught it in his palm and squeezed—hard—until Sara yelped.

"You will quit this and behave. Now! I don't want to kill you but I will if you don't cease this tantrum at once." He punctuated his words by tightening his hold even more, until she could feel the bones grinding against each other under the intense pressure being exerted on them.

"Fuck you," Sara said through clenched teeth.

"I had planned to wait until we were elsewhere but if you insist..." he mocked her. He pushed against her until her back met the resistance of a tree, its rough bark biting into her flesh through the thin cotton of her pajamas. One clawed hand gripped both of her wrists and raised them above her head. A thick thigh forced its way between hers.

Sara struggled against him. "You'll have to kill me first, you bastard!"

"No, I don't think I'll kill you. I'll fuck you. I will breed you. But I won't kill you. It'll be so much more entertaining to make you my whore." He leaned in closer and licked the side of her face, his disgusting black tongue leaving a slimy path on her skin. Sara whimpered in fear and tried to turn her face away. He caught her chin with his claw and forced her to face him, their eyes only inches apart. "What do you think of that? Think you'll like being my whore?"

Sara reared her head back and spit at him, the shiny saliva splattering over his chin. "I would rather die."

Smiling, he wiped the moisture from his face. The evil glow behind his reptilian eyes grew brighter. "We'll see," he said, the malicious intent in his voice causing her to tremble. "Now where was I? Oh yes, now I remember. We were discussing your other request."

"You're going to let me go?" Sara knew the answer before the words had finished leaving her mouth. *Stupid. Stupid. Stupid.*

"No. I'm going to fuck you." His claw cut through the straps of her pajamas like they were butter. The top fell down around her waist, baring her breasts to the cold night air. His gaze dropped to her chest, where her nipples sprang up, tight and hard. "Now look at that. Deny wanting me all you like, but your body knows what it was made for."

Roughly, he pinched and twisted her nipple. Pain shot through her body. Sara clenched her teeth as hard as she could, determined to show the monster no weakness. She wanted to shriek, to call out for Mark, but couldn't. Mark was no match for this creature's unholy strength. She'd only be putting them both in danger. Better that one of them was left behind to take care of Sam. Tears spilled down her cheeks at the thought of being taken away from her son, never seeing him grow into the wonderful young man she knew he would become.

The beast moved against her, the threat of his arousal prodding at the juncture between her legs. She could hardly contain the cry of fear trying to burst free. Sara bit into her lip, the coppery taste of blood filling her mouth.

Movement to her right caught her eye. A twig snapped, causing the beast to turn. Sara took advantage of the momentary diversion to scream for all she was worth. "Help!"

The man/creature roared, clamping his hand over her mouth and nose, cutting off her oxygen. "Take a good look around you, Sara. There's no help coming for you. You belong to me."

Sara bit down on his hand, desperate for air. When he jerked it back, she took great gulps of oxygen into her lungs and hissed at him with what little breath she possessed. "I'll never belong to you, you freak of nature."

"You're mine. *Mine!*"

His palm shoved her head back into the tree's bark. Light exploded behind her eyes. Pain raced from the point of impact into her neck and shoulders, so severe in its intensity that her stomach rolled and churned.

Sharp teeth sank into the soft flesh of her throat. Agony that made childbirth seem like a bee sting ripped through her. The horrified scream Sara managed to contain earlier burst free and echoed through the trees surrounding her.

୨୦୦୧

Long after he left the house, Tristan sat in his car. His head resting on the steering wheel, he tried to psychoanalyze why saying goodbye hadn't granted him the closure he'd expected. A bloodcurdling scream tore through the quiet neighborhood. He raised his head, hitting it against the roof with a resounding thump.

Sara.

He was out of the car and barreling his way up the front walk before his hand reached back for the semi-automatic usually tucked into the back of his waistband. When his fingers met the soft denim covering his ass, he cursed. He'd left his damn weapon at the apartment. Without it, he felt naked. He leaned forward and pulled out the small knife he kept inside his boot. It wasn't much but it would have to do.

A dog barked from somewhere around the back of the house and Tristan stopped to listen. When it came again, he veered around the side of the building, careful to stay in the shadows, and hustled toward where he perceived the sound to have come from.

An animal howled in the distance, causing a foreboding chill to chase down his spine. *God damn it.* He couldn't see anything, but something was up. He was sure of it. He would be damned if he was going to go before he figured out what it was.

He followed the sound of the dog's wail into the wooded area behind the house. Each step made him feel a little more like a fool. He began to think his imagination had conjured the scream, his subconscious fabricating it as an excuse to keep him from leaving.

A twig snapped ahead of him, dry leaves crackled. Someone or something was out there. It was probably just the dog he'd heard, but he needed to know for sure. Tristan crept closer.

A couple stood braced against an old oak tree, making out. Jesus, he really was getting old if he couldn't tell the difference between a woman's cry of pleasure from one of pain. Disgusted with himself he started to leave, to give the couple their privacy, when something odd caught his attention.

It wasn't much, mainly the woman's posture, the way she held herself, her arms hanging limply at her sides. The man's bulky body pressed up against her tightly, blocking her from Tristan's view.

The moon chose that precise moment to peek out from behind the clouds, highlighting the pair better than a spotlight. It was enough for Tristan to make out a few of the woman's features. Pure unadulterated rage rushed through him. Years of intense training and conditioning disappeared to be replaced by primitive instincts he hadn't known he possessed. All he knew was that the woman trapped against the tree was his woman. She was his, and he had to get to her, save her before it was too late.

Breaking into a dead run, Tristan prayed to a God he hadn't spoken to in years that he would make it to her in time. His fist tightened around the hilt of the knife in his hand, his knuckles turning white under the pressure.

He reached them just as Sara's attacker began to raise his head, revealing a mouthful of serrated, bloody teeth. Tristan plunged his knife to the hilt in the side of the vampire's throat. The abomination roared in pain and fury, letting go of Sara to swipe back at Tristan with cruel, razor-sharp claws. Sara's unconscious body slid down the tree and crumpled at his feet.

The vampire turned, Sara's blood dripping from its chin, and hissed, rushing at Tristan. He jumped to the side, but was too late. The vampire slammed into him, the impact sending them both hurdling backward. At the last possible second, Tristan rolled to his side, putting himself on top. The vampire hit the ground with an oomph, air gushing from his lungs under the impact. Tristan used the momentary lapse of movement to his advantage, his fists pumping hard and fast into the monster's deformed face. Claws rose and began to rip into his chest and slash at his face. Tristan felt nothing. He was blind, deaf and dumb to his own pain, to everything except his goal to kill the creature below him and get to Sara, take care of her.

He spared a second to glance her way and worried that she appeared much too pale, and far too still. If he didn't hurry, there was a good chance she wouldn't survive.

The beast surged up beneath him, attacking with renewed vigor. It slashed out, knocking Tristan to his back. The thing forged up and straddled Tristan's chest, trapping his arms to his sides. *No!* He was not going to lose this fight. His life didn't matter but he had to save Sara. He bucked his hips and swung his legs upward, catching the creature's head between his feet. His calf muscles straining, he flipped their positions. Once again with the upper hand, Tristan grabbed the knife protruding from the vampire's neck and pushed with all his weight, sending the blade careening clear through to the other side. Blood splattered his clothes and face.

He shoved the creature away, satisfied with the lifeless flop the body gave against the cold, hard ground. He left it there, lying in a pool of its own blood, and hurried to Sara

Please, God, let her be okay!

He searched frantically for a pulse, careful of the gaping wound on her neck that already appeared to be healing at the edges. After several nervous seconds he finally located a weak and unsteady beat under his fingers. Whatever the vampire's intent, he hadn't meant to kill her. Without conscious thought, the healing properties in his saliva wouldn't have been deployed and she would have already bled to death.

She was alive. His eyes misted over in relief. She was hurt but hanging on. Always a fighter, Sara would make it. He brushed her hair tenderly away from her pallid face and pressed a gentle kiss to her forehead before turning back to finish decapitating the vampire.

His eyes widened when he found only a pool of congealed blood on the forest floor. The creature was gone. His attention returned to Sara as a gruesome realization struck him. The creature had drank from Sara, ingesting her blood. That meant there was a good chance they would be psychically linked. The monster would be able to track her, find her no matter where she hid. The bastard would be back. There was no doubt in Tristan's mind about that. As soon as the vampire healed, he would come looking for Sara to finish what he'd started. By letting Sara heal, the vampire had made his intentions clear. Whatever his plans for her, whether it was to cross her over and make her his companion or keep her as a blood slave, the vampire had put his claim on Sara. Tristan vowed not to let it come to that. Neither the puppet masters who held claim to his life, nor the supernatural forces at work, would keep him from protecting what was his. And whether she knew it or not, Sara still belonged to him. No more harm would come to her.

He swept Sara up in his arms. Holding her close to his heart, he carried her toward his waiting car.

Chapter Seven

"No!" Sara came up fighting, her arms and legs scissoring. A panicked whimper flew from her mouth. The same inky darkness from the dream surrounded her but as sleep faded she could feel the soft comfort of the bed beneath her.

A dream...

It had all been a bad dream. She was home, safely tucked away in her own bed.

There was no such thing as monsters.

She flopped back against the mattress and cuddled the fluffy pillow to her chest, her heart still racing from the nightmare. She reached for Mark, wanting to burrow up against his sleep-warmed body and feel something real, something that would help chase away the lingering horror. To Sara's disappointment, all she felt was the bed, cold and empty, underneath her outstretched hand.

Where was Mark?

Footsteps sounded outside the bedroom. Sara waited, expecting Mark to come in and crawl into bed next to her. She'd probably scared him half to death, screaming the way she had. Thankfully, Sam was a sound sleeper, or she would have woken him up too. She was glad for that. She didn't want her frequent night terrors to bother her son.

Sara sat up and ran a hand through her mussed hair, pushing it behind her ears. A twinge of pain shot through her neck as she brushed over it. She returned to touch the spot that hurt, her fingers gently tracing over it. A patch of skin between her neck and shoulder felt tight and bruised, like a recently healed scar. One that shouldn't be there. *What in the...?*

The bedroom door flung open, bouncing hard off the wall behind it with a loud crack. The overhead light flared to life. Temporarily blinded, Sara closed her eyes and raised her arm to block the harsh light. "Mark, turn off the light. And for God's sake don't be so loud. Sam's a deep sleeper, but he won't sleep through racket like that."

"Sorry to disappoint you, darling. Mark isn't here."

That voice... Her eyes flew open and her mouth gaped. Sara barely noticed her strange surroundings as her vision tunneled, centering on the man in front of her. She slammed her eyelids shut, squeezing them tight.

Just a hallucination. He wasn't really there.

Sara counted to ten, then just to be on the safe side, continued on to twenty, before taking a second look.

He didn't disappear. He was still there staring back at her, as big as life and twice as real. His hair was longer than she remembered, and pulled back from his chiseled face with a rubber band. His lean cheeks were covered with a couple of days' worth of dark stubble that normally made her think of bad personal grooming. On him it looked dangerous and sexy.

Sara stared, her mouth hanging open far enough to catch flies. She probably looked like a buffoon, but couldn't summon the will to care. She wanted to soak it all in, absorb and memorize every inch of his masculine body.

Tristan leaned against the doorjamb, his heavily muscled arms crossed over the broad expanse of his hairy chest. Threadbare jogging pants rode low on his trim hips, concealing the lower half of his magnificent body from her appreciative gaze. It didn't, however, manage to hide the growing bulge between his legs. The longer she stared, the bigger it got, as if it could feel her attention and was trying to show off. Sara licked her parched lips.

She slowly made the return trip back up his body. This time she picked up the scars and imperfections she missed on first inspection. None of it mattered. Even the jagged, puckered scar that slashed across his chest from collarbone to slightly above one flat copper nipple didn't detract from his appeal. Somehow it only made him appear more attractive, more feral.

Her body responded to the sight of him. Her nipples puckered and strained against the soft cotton nightshirt she wore. Her pussy grew moist and clenched emptily. Whether her mind was in agreement or not, her body was revving up for action.

If this was another dream, she didn't want to ever wake up.

At last, she let her gaze meet his, wary of what she would find there. Pale blue met forest green and clashed, reigniting the fire in her soul that had been reduced to ash in his absence.

Sara gasped, visibly shaken from the jolt. "Tristan...?"

He stalked over to the bed. There was no other way to describe the sinuous way he moved toward her, as smooth and lethal as a panther tracking its prey. He stopped and sank down on the mattress, hip to hip beside her, so close she could feel the heat coming off him in waves, smell a hint of soap clinging to his skin and the heady underlying male musk that was his alone.

Lightly, she touched his face, her fingers whispering over his jaw for a split second before jerking back. Sara couldn't help but notice the heat filling his eyes in response to her touch. It only lasted an instant before disappearing to be replaced with a softer expression, one she couldn't identify. Embarrassed, she could only guess at the reason behind the gentle look. Apparently, he too had noticed how badly her hand trembled as she'd touched him.

A scary thought occurred to her and she blurted it out loud. "Am I dead?"

Tristan wrapped his arms around her, hugging her to him. "No, baby, you're not dead." His voice was deep and rough, filled with emotion.

Sara pressed her face against his chest, rubbing her nose into the fine hair growing between his pecs, and held onto him. She inhaled, taking his scent deep into her lungs. Her arms tightened around him like a vise. It felt so good to have him there, in her arms, after so long. "But...how can you be here?" For the first time she looked at the room around them. The bare walls and peeling wallpaper didn't give her any hints about where she was. "Where exactly is here?"

"I brought you back to the apartment," he said, as if that explained everything. He swallowed, his Adam's apple bobbing. "You're in my bedroom." Sara felt his muscles tense. "My bed."

Sara gulped nervously when he pulled back, his gaze easing over her, igniting every inch of skin it lingered on. What she wouldn't give for it to be his hands, mouth, tongue touching her with the same undisguised lust.

Her hand settled over his heart, his muscles rigid beneath her touch. Sara marveled at the strong and steady thump she felt beneath her palm. Tristan was alive. How many times had she cried herself to sleep wishing for that very thing? There were so many questions she needed to ask him, things she needed to tell him, but she wouldn't. Not now. They could play twenty questions later, after the clawing ache deep inside her had been sated. She didn't dare ruin the beautiful opportunity she'd been given.

It didn't matter where he'd been or that he'd been gone for so long, or how he was able to be with her now. The only thing that mattered was that she loved him. The intensity of how much frightened her. She'd loved Tristan for what felt like her entire life, a love that even death hadn't wavered. Sara wanted to experience the ultimate expression of love with him. Wanted to be with Tristan more than she wanted to see her next sunrise. Against all odds, they were together and she wasn't about to let the chance of a lifetime pass her by. She'd been accused of a lot of things in her life but being a fool wasn't one of them.

Opening her mouth to tell him as much, she was silenced when his mouth crushed over hers, stealing her words, causing a rush of pleasure so sweet it literally took her breath. Sara moaned her compliance and licked along the seam of his lips, begging for him to deepen the kiss.

Tristan's hungry growl spurred her on, made her feel reckless and sexy, boosted her confidence. Her fingers traveled around his neck and buried themselves in the crisp hair at his nape, pulling him closer. She licked him again and was rewarded by his tongue coming out to play, rubbing and thrusting against her own, mimicking the act she so desperately wanted.

She drew him in, sucking on the velvety length of his tongue, and savored the delicious taste of him. She couldn't get enough. His flavor seeped into her pores. Set her on fire.

His heavy frame pushed her down into the soft mattress. Sara spread her legs wide and wrapped them around his waist. He settled against her, the steely length of his erection pressing into the vee between her thighs. "Oh yes," she groaned as he ground his hardness into the soft mound of her pussy.

Something didn't feel right, or maybe it was that something felt *too* right. Although she wore the same kind of T-shirt she usually slept in, she was naked beneath it. Only the thin material of his sweatpants stood between them, separating his cock from where she ached for it to be.

She gripped his ass and pressed tighter against him. Sneaky fingers delved beneath fabric to caress him. His ass was fantastic, all firm muscle and hot, silky skin. She wanted to pinch it, break free and take a bite out of it. If she wasn't so happy to be exactly where she was, she might have. Later, she promised herself.

"Oh God, Sara. I've missed you so much, baby," Tristan breathed next to her ear, his mouth nipping her earlobe. Sara arched her hips, rotating them against him, egging him on. He groaned, shuddering against her. "You have no idea how good it feels to hold you."

Sara had no time to respond, no time to think, as Tristan's mouth moved over her skin. He traveled from one tender spot to the next, his mouth a deadly weapon of seduction.

Scalding wet heat engulfed her cotton-covered nipple. Sara gasped and inhaled a deep, ragged breath of air. Tristan bit down gently, sucking the turgid bud into his mouth. Liquid lightning raced from her breast to the center of her sex, leaving her wet and empty, the walls of her pussy clenching in need. Her back arched, pressing her breasts harder against him, telling him without words what she needed. More.

Calloused hands worked under the soft nightshirt and started to drag it up her body. His mouth left her nipple to follow the trail of skin he uncovered. Sara whimpered at the loss. "Patience, baby. I want to feel you naked against me."

"Patience my ass, Tristan." The simple act of saying his name aloud sent a spear of longing to her core. "It's been too long. I want you inside me. Now."

Sara followed the lean line of his waist around his body until her palm rested against the firm jut of his erection. She pumped her fist around him once and again, loving the way he pulsed and grew larger, harder, in her grip.

Tristan groaned low in his throat and thrust his hips back at her, his cock pushing against her hand for more. Instead of giving him the hard stroke she knew he wanted, she released him and moved her hand lower, to caress the tightly drawn sack beneath, her fingers whispering over the fragile, wrinkled skin.

Sara wanted to tease him. To make him as crazy with desire as he made her.

A growl vibrated in Tristan's chest seconds before it erupted from his lips. In the blink of an eye, she found herself face down on the bed, a pillow shoved beneath her hips, her naked ass in the air.

She heard him moving behind her. Could hear drawers opening and closing, as if he searched for something. Never one to be patient, she turned to see what he was up to. Tristan's warm hands pressed into her back, pinning her to the bed. "Ah, ah, ah," he whispered, his breath fanning against her neck and sending shivers of want down her spine. "Curiosity killed the cat."

"Fuck you," she said, her voice more amused than angry.

"All in good time, princess. I think I'll take my nice sweet time playing with your sexy body." He punctuated his words by running the flat of his tongue down her spine all the way to the dimple above her bottom. "You're as delicious as I remember. Mmm..." he groaned, "...maybe more. I know the next part of you I want to taste." Fingers dipping lower, he traced the hollow between her buttocks around to the wet folds of her pussy, where Sara frothed in need for him.

"Damn it, Tristan, stop playing and fuck me already. I'm dying up here," she pleaded, wiggling her pussy against his fingers, trying to get him to touch her where she wanted.

Tristan chuckled, his deep throaty laugh turning her on more. Her thighs were awash in her desire for him. "All in good time," he repeated. "First I need you to do something for me."

"Anything."

"Anything?"

"Yes, damn it!"

"I like the sound of that. Shut your eyes for me, princess."

Sara shut her eyes and waited to see what he would do next, the suspense killing her.

A soft piece of fabric grazed her cheek. Sara turned her face into his touch. Her hair was lifted from her neck and draped over one shoulder. A piece of cloth was then loosely wrapped around her neck.

"Trust me?"

"Yes," Sara whispered. Tristan moved the cloth up and over her eyes, securing it in a knot at the back of her head. A blindfold.

Lifting her face, Sara pursed her lips, hoping he was still looking at her face and would notice what she was doing, what she needed him to do to reassure her. He did. His lips closed over hers in a tender kiss. Warm breath fanned over her face as he pulled back, her bottom lip trapped between his. He drew it into his mouth and lightly sucked on it. Images of him doing the same to her nipples, her clit, arose and she moaned, anxious for her fantasies to be realized.

Sara followed his lead when he lifted her up onto her knees, pulling the shirt over her head. Naked, she sat trembling with desire for him and awaited his next move. Not knowing what he was going to do excited her. She wondered if he had lost the sweatpants yet, if he was as naked as she was. "Are you going to get rid of those pants?"

"They're already gone, baby."

He lifted her hand, guiding it to his erection. Sara wrapped her fingers around his considerable girth and began to slowly stroke up and down his shaft. The pad of her thumb ran over the flared rim of his cock, found moisture and spread it over the crown. When more liquid oozed under her gentle coaxing, she brought her fingers to her mouth and began to lick his essence off her skin. Salty and delicious, his flavor burst over her palate.

She could feel his gaze on her as she cleaned each finger in turn, one after another, wanting more of him. She wanted to take him in her mouth and love him as only she could.

"I love the way you taste. Let me suck your cock. I want you to come in my mouth." Her words rang with the longing she'd felt for years and been denied.

His hands landed on her shoulders and he lowered Sara to her back, her head hanging precariously close to the edge of the bed. Body heat rolled off him as he inched closer. The spongy tip of his erection rubbed over her lips and Sara opened wide. Like a baby bird in search of sustenance, she pulled the tip of him into her mouth and bathed the swollen crown in wet heat, laving away the small trace of pre-come she discovered. Tristan moaned, his hips shifting against her, forcing his cock deeper into her mouth. Sara relaxed her jaw and accepted as much of him as she could take. She used her lips, teeth and palate to massage his swollen flesh while her tongue swirled all around him. Sara loved this. The sense of empowerment she got from the simple act was awing. She was in control of his pleasure. She could give him the heights of passion or bring him to his knees in pain.

Sara chose pleasure. He hit the back of her throat and she swallowed, relaxing her throat muscles and taking him in farther. Only when she felt his balls slap against her chin was she satisfied. She swallowed, over and over, breathing through her nose as she flexed her throat around the head of his cock.

She felt him harden a degree more and braced herself for his climax, wanting to savor him when he finally came. His balls drew up tight against his body and she knew he was almost there.

At the last second, Tristan pulled back, his penis leaving her mouth with a resounding pop.

"Tristan?" Sara clumsily sat up, her hand automatically going to the blindfold. She wanted it off so that she would be able to see his face, read what was in his eyes. He stilled her hand before she could remove the material.

"There's no way I'm coming in your mouth, not when I can come buried deep inside your tight pussy." Tristan's voice sounded strange, filled with a hodgepodge of different emotions, none of which she could identify because they were all mixed in there together.

"Do it then," Sara said. "Make love with me." She was so turned-on she knew she would come as soon as he entered her. One hard thrust would finish her off. Sara reached for him, her hand extended out in the empty air. A loud noise, a door slamming, drew her up short. Her hands flew back to her chest, covering her breasts.

Tristan cursed and pulled the blindfold from her face. "We've got company." Sara blinked up at him, her pupils adjusting to the change in light. She watched as he tugged on a pair of faded blue jeans and a black T-shirt.

He turned to her with another black shirt and a pair of drawstring jogging pants. "Sorry, it's the best I can do right now. I don't think any of my other clothes will work."

Sara picked up the clothes he dropped in front of her and stared back at him owlishly. Why couldn't they have had just a little more time together before reality had to intrude and ruin it?

"Hurry and dress. There's a bathroom right behind you if you want to clean up first. Make it quick though."

A great sense of impending doom closed around her, squeezing her heart in a tight vise, making it difficult to breathe, to think. Bitter tears rushed to the surface, filling her eyes, and Sara blinked them away before he noticed.

"Tristan, there's something I have to tell you. It's really important. You need to know about..." *Sam.* She had to tell him about their son, now, before anything else happened. Before fate or destiny, or whoever the hell kept screwing up her life, took Tristan away from her again.

"Later, Sara. We don't have the time right now." He hustled her off the bed and into the bathroom, shutting the door behind her before she had the chance to say anything else.

Sara pulled on the clothes and tried to make her hair lay down on her head. Not an easy thing to do when the only tool she could find to run through her tangled hair was a comb missing half its bristles. After going through the drawers under the sink she found a plain rubber band and pulled her hair into a sloppy ponytail.

Satisfied that she'd done the best she could, she splashed cold water on her face and stared at her reflection. Her gaze wandered down her neck, a garish blue and purple bruise catching her attention. She twisted her neck, inspecting it from all angles. How had she done that?

Just like that, the night before came back to her in shocking detail. She gripped the sink, her fingers biting into the cheap, white porcelain in an effort to steady herself. A debilitating wave of nausea hit her and she leaned over, heaving white foam into the basin. She wiped her lips with the back of her hand and turned on the faucet, rinsing her mouth of the bitter bile, before raising her head to gape at her reflection. How had she come through the attack so unscathed? The last thing she recalled was being bitten, the searing heat of teeth sinking into her throat. In disbelief, her hand rose and fingered the nasty bruise on her neck. By all rights, she should be dead, instead of standing in a strange apartment, marveling over Tristan being alive and well.

Oh my God, Mark and Sam were still at the house. She had been begging Tristan to make love to her while her family was in danger.

Sara raced out of the bathroom and ran face first into Tristan's broad chest. "You have to take me home! Sam and Mark are still there. They could be in danger. You have to—"

"You have to calm down," Tristan interrupted, his arms folding around her in a protective hug.

Damn it, why wouldn't he let her explain? "No! You don't understand—"

"I do. I do understand, but you don't have anything to worry about. Sam and Mark are perfectly safe. I had Shame watch over the house last night and told him to bring them by here first thing this morning. That was the company I was talking about."

His words calmed Sara. Sam and Mark were safe. They were here. *Oh my God, they're here.*

She jerked free of Tristan's embrace, flying through the door and down the hallway, her only thought of getting to her son and Mark before Tristan did. The short hall opened up into a living room. There was an ugly floral sofa and an older-model television sitting on an end table. Other than that, the room was empty. She stepped inside, confused about where her family was supposed to be, if not here, and heard a rustling noise to her right. She spun around to see a strange man with a vicious scowl on his face stalking toward her from another doorway she'd neglected to notice. The way he held his powerful body told her that he wasn't a man she wanted to cross. Even from across the room, she could feel the force of his presence. He reminded her of the wild animals she had watched on the Discovery Channel, ready to pounce at the slightest provocation.

Sara's brain screamed out a warning, telling her to run. Her feet wouldn't move. She just stood frozen where she was, like a lamb ready for slaughter, and whimpered.

Warm hands landed on Sara's shoulders from behind. "Sara, meet my partner, Shame."

"He's Shame?" she asked in disbelief. "He's the man you said you left to watch over Sam and Mark?"

Tristan's partner leaned against the fridge and cocked a dark red eyebrow at them. "Hey, I'm right here. You don't have to talk around me like I'm simple or something."

Sara cast him a quick glance beneath her lashes and turned back to Tristan. "I thought you said he would bring them back here with him?"

"So I did," Tristan replied before turning to the other man. "You want to explain to the lady why her son and fiancé aren't here with you like they're supposed to be?"

Sara couldn't help but notice the way he practically spit out the word fiancé. It almost sounded like he was jealous. Her ego soared at the thought but something else, some other emotion she couldn't identify, nudged at the back of her conscience. Guilt. She'd almost slept with Tristan while planning to marry Mark. And worse, she didn't regret it. She wasn't in love with Mark and he knew it. Mark's knowledge of her feelings didn't help relieve the guilt though.

But if Tristan knew about her engagement, what else did he know? Surely if he had looked into her life that much then he would know about Sam. If that was the case then he wasn't the man she thought he was. The one she remembered and loved. That Tristan would never have ignored the fact that he had a child.

Any man who would deny their parentage made her sick. Reminded her all too well of the bastard who had fathered her and promptly abandoned her and her mother for his career, leaving them alone to fend for themselves.

"I tried to get them to come, but the dude wouldn't even hear me out. As soon as I mentioned Tristan's name he freaked and slammed the door in my face. What did you want me to do, break down the door and drag them out?"

"Jesus, Shame." Tristan reached over Sara's shoulder and slapped Shame in the head. "Mark thought I was dead. No wonder he freaked out."

"Will somebody just tell me what the hell is going on here?" Sara looked from one man to the other. Neither said anything, apparently surprised that she had yelled at them. The look on their faces would have amused her if she wasn't so pissed and confused and worried and...who the hell was she kidding, other than confused, she didn't know what she was feeling.

"Sara," Tristan said gently, "I'll explain everything to you, but not now. Let me get a few things together and we'll go over to your place and check on things. Then we can have a nice long talk, okay?"

How dare he talk down to her? "No. You're going to tell me what I want to know and you're going to do it right now. And don't speak to me like I'm some child you have to placate. I won't have it. Do you hear me?"

Shame gave her a mock salute. "Yes, ma'am." His face looked serious but she heard the laughter in his voice. It grated on her nerves.

Tristan hugged her close, his arms tight around her waist. "When we get to your house, Sara. Then I'll tell you what I can."

Chapter Eight

I must be a masochist. It was the only explanation Tristan could find for why he was in Sara's house, watching her flit back and forth between her family and his partner like some damn social butterfly, trying to make sure everyone was okay. Everyone except him, that is. Him she avoided like the plague. She wouldn't even look him in the eye for God's sake.

Not that he was letting it bother him. He relaxed his fingers, forcing them out of the stiff fists he'd unconsciously balled them into. The fact that she was doing her level best to ignore him wasn't getting to him at all. He was used to being the odd man out. The person always on the outside looking in.

"Don't you think it's about time we get this show on the road, man?"

Shame's voice startled Tristan as his partner came up behind him. He'd been so engrossed in Sara's movements, watching the way she interacted with her son...their son, that he hadn't heard his partner's approach. "Yeah," Tristan grunted in reply. He was as ready as he was ever going to be.

He walked over to where Sara sat, playing with Sam, and touched her shoulder. "We need to have that talk now, Sara." Her eyes widened and she cast a frantic glance at the boy. It was obvious she didn't want anything to be said in front of him.

On that score, they were in complete agreement. "Shame will take him up to his room and keep him occupied while we talk if you want. Maybe Mark could—"

"I'm not leaving Sara. I have just as much right to hear what you're going to say as she does." Mark's angry voice rang out, interrupting him. It was the first time he'd said a word to Tristan since they'd arrived.

Tristan straightened, looking Mark in the eye. "I was only going to suggest that you help them get settled so Sam would feel more comfortable with Shame. I may not know much about kids but I thought he might be more comfortable around Shame if you showed him it was okay."

"And whose fault is it that you don't know much about your own kid?"

Sara gasped. "Mark!"

Tristan ignored Mark's barb and looked imploringly at Shame. He came right over and squatted down close to Sam, a friendly smile on his face. Within minutes he had the little boy giggling at something he'd said and was swinging him up onto his broad shoulders for a piggyback ride. The twinge of jealousy Tristan felt at how easily Shame won his son over was unexpected and unwanted. He stood, waiting until they were out of hearing range before facing Sara and Mark and the inquisition to come. They had a right to answers, but he was at a loss for where to begin.

"So how are we going to do this?" Sara looked from Mark, sitting beside her on the sofa, to Tristan, who sat in one of the two rocking chairs across from them.

"Simple," Tristan answered. "You ask the questions and I'll answer what I can."

"Okay," Sara replied, nervously running her palms up and down the length of her denim-covered thighs.

Tristan swallowed. "Before we begin, you should know that there will be some questions I can't answer. It's for your own safety."

"Bullshit," Mark piped in. "What's next? You going to tell us that you could tell us, but then you'd have to kill us?"

Since his smart-ass comment was closer to the truth than Tristan wanted to admit, he skirted around it. "You're just going to have to accept that you can't know everything."

"Why?" Sara's gaze was filled with questions when it finally settled on his face. "I don't understand."

Tristan met Sara's eyes. "Just know that I would tell you everything if I could." He owed her the truth. He didn't owe Mark a damn thing.

Mark shot him a smug look and wrapped his arm around Sara's back, giving her shoulder a squeeze. Sara probably thought the action was meant for comfort. Tristan knew differently. It was a possessive demonstration for his behalf alone.

He wondered how fast he could wipe the condescending smile off the bastard's face if he informed him of where Sara had spent the night. Told him that she had been in his bed, in his arms, moaning for his touch only a short time ago.

"All right. Whatever you say, Tristan." Sara sighed. "I'd like to get this over with. The sooner we can get this whole mess sorted out and put behind us the better."

Tristan heard the unspoken meaning behind her words loud and clear. The quicker he disappeared, the happier she would be.

"Fine by me," he snapped. "Ask your questions." A hurt look crossed over Sara's face, making him instantly regret his tone. This couldn't be easy on her, and he wasn't making things any more pleasant by acting like an ass. He rephrased his question and gentled his tone. "What do you want to know first?"

Sara's gaze darted back and forth between him and Mark, like she wasn't sure she should ask whatever it was on her mind. Her lashes lowered and her breasts heaved under the force of her breath. She shot an apologetic look at Mark before speaking. "You're supposed to be dead," she whispered, so low he had to lean forward and strain to make out her words. "Since you're obviously alive and well, I want to know why. Why all the lies? If you wanted to get rid of me and move on to greener pastures, all you had to do was say so. You didn't have to fake your own death to do it. Why did you want us to think you were dead?"

One lone tear streamed down her cheek. Tristan felt her anguish like a punch in the gut. He expected her to ask where the hell he'd been, rail at him for leaving. Anger he could deal with. He didn't know how to cope with the hurt and sorrow, or her assumption that he'd faked his death to get rid of her. It was the farthest thing from the truth. "I'm sorry, Sara. I can't answer most of that. I can tell you that I didn't want to leave. The choice was taken out my hands." Both she and Mark looked at him in doubt.

Mark snorted. "Okay. Where have you been all this time and why are you back now?"

Tristan turned to answer Mark's question, expecting to see the anger and loathing that had been directed at him since he'd walked in the door. Instead he saw that Sara hadn't been the only one to suffer at his loss.

While anger still clouded Mark's face, grief was there as well. That he'd never considered Mark being hurt by his leaving or really caring one way or the other after his disappearance made him feel like scum. It was a feeling he seemed to be experiencing a lot lately.

Once upon a time they'd been close. As close as two misfit orphans could be. They were both placed into the same foster home when he was sixteen. For two years they'd lived together as quasi-brothers. He felt like a real bastard for not considering that Mark may have been hurt by his disappearance.

He looked at the couple across from him with newly opened eyes. How could he stay angry at both of them for coming together in their grief over losing him? It was his fault they were together.

Tristan met Mark's inquisitive stare. "I'm sorry. I can't tell you that either. As for why I'm here, Shame and I have been looking into the string of murders in this area lately. I guess you could say we were hired to investigate The Mangler."

"I want to know one more thing and then we can move on to what happened last night." Sara chewed on her bottom lip, her gaze raking over his face. "I expect a damn answer this time, Tristan. So help me God, if you don't give me one, I won't be responsible for my actions."

"I'll answer if I can, Sara. That's all I can promise. There are some things I don't have the ability to tell you." He watched her fidget around in her seat for a moment before she spoke.

"Did you know about Sam?"

"Jesus Christ, Sara," he said, sitting back forcefully against the chair as if she had reached out and slapped him. "No, I didn't know. Of course I didn't. I only found out about him earlier this week, when I came back to town. If you believe a single damn word that comes out of my mouth, you should believe that."

The relief he saw cross over her features stung. Did she really think he would have abandoned his own child? That he was no better than the scum who abandoned him when he was a kid?

Sara tilted her head, studying his face. "Okay, I believe you." She bit her lip. "So what exactly are we dealing with here? What the hell was that thing that attacked me last night?"

"A vampire," Tristan said bluntly.

Mark sat forward. "Bullshit! There's no such thing as vampires."

"It's not bullshit, Mark. If you'd been up close and personal with that...thing, like I was, you wouldn't doubt his words either. Whatever it was...is, I already knew it wasn't human." Her eyes glazed over, a faraway expression on her face. Shivers racked her petite body. Sympathy and love warred inside Tristan. He burned to take her in his arms and hold her, wipe the horrific memory away. He wanted to be the one who pulled her into his arms and soothed away her fears. Instead he got to sit alone, within reaching distance of her, and watch Mark do it.

The bitter taste of jealousy filled his mouth.

"How did I end up with you last night? The last thing I remember was being attacked. It shoved me up against a tree and I thought I was done for, then nothing. Not until I woke up in your...at your place."

Her cheeks flushed a pretty shade of pink at her slip-up. He knew she was going to say "in your bed" but had changed her mind at the last minute. He wondered if she was thinking about what had happened between them before Shame had come back and interrupted. He sure as hell couldn't think of anything else.

"I was here," Tristan admitted. "Or rather I was outside. I came to see Sam, and heard you scream. I pulled the thing off of you and tried to kill it. I thought it was dead when I turned to check on you but when I looked back it was gone."

Sara's eyes widened. "You came to see Sam?"

Inwardly, Tristan winced. Of all the things for her to focus on she had to pick that one.

"What did you think you were going to accomplish by coming to see a five-year-old kid in the middle of the night? It's not like he would be awake at that hour," Mark said.

Sara answered for him. "He wasn't going to knock on the door and wait to be invited in. Were you?" She looked at him accusingly.

"No," he murmured.

"So..." Sara changed the subject. "What else do I need to know?"

"Several things. First of all there are a few details you should know about the creature that attacked you. I'm not talking about the same creature from popular horror movies. It's not charming or romantic. He's not allergic to daylight or garlic. Unless they choose otherwise, a vampire doesn't look any different than you or I. They could be your friend, your neighbor. Most of what the two of you think you know about this creature is nothing more than myth and superstition. This is the real deal and it's still out there...somewhere." Tristan paused, giving them a minute to absorb what he'd said. "When he bit you, he infected you with his saliva. There may be some unpleasant side effects."

"What kind of side effects?" both she and Mark asked at the same time.

Tristan didn't want to scare her but there was no easy way to explain what she needed to know. "When a vampire drinks from someone, especially this type of vampire, it forms a link with them. A sort of psychic connection."

Mark interrupted him again. "Give me a break, man. This is fucking ridiculous. It's like I've stepped into a warped episode of

The Twilight Zone or something." He ran his hands over his face and released a long, exasperated breath of air. "So you're telling us there's more than one kind of vampire?"

"Yes," Tristan answered him. "Now if I could continue?"

"Yeah...yeah, go ahead."

Tristan turned his attention back to Sara. "Another side effect is your healing. You were hurt pretty bad last night. He took a good-sized chunk out of the side of your throat."

As long as he lived Tristan would never forget his terror at seeing her like that, all pale and lifeless on the cold ground. The fear that she wouldn't make it. That he wouldn't be able to help her.

"There are healing properties in a vampire's saliva. Thanks to those properties you were pretty much healed by the time you woke up. I'm sure you noticed the tender spot on your neck where he fed from you. That means that you're probably going to have some visions or brief flashes of him, see things through his eyes. You'll see whatever he's doing at the time they hit you. It won't be fun, but we might be able to use them to our advantage. Shame and I can use your connection with him to track him down and finish him off."

Sara sat back against the couch. Her face had lost all of its color, her expression bleak. "So in a nutshell, you're saying that this thing...this vampire drank my blood and now I'm going to start having all these crazy flashbacks or whatever."

Tristan nodded.

"Jesus," Mark huffed. "This sounds like the plot for a bad horror movie."

Mark's eyes were wide and his voice had a hysterical edge to it that wasn't promising. Tristan knew Mark was trying to accept the reality of the situation but they didn't have time to spare while he gradually came to grips with it. He needed to have the reality of the situation slapped right in his face. Schooling his features into the calm mask he wore when hunting, Tristan spoke quietly, his voice all the more deadly because of its soft cadence. "This isn't a movie. It doesn't get any more real than this."

His jaw firmed as he looked at the other man, once his friend, now his replacement. The pity he wanted to feel for Mark wouldn't come. "Suck it up, man. Sara needs you. The sooner you realize that the better."

Tristan cast a coveted look toward Sara, who was curled into a ball on the far end of the sofa, her knees pulled underneath her chin, her bottom lip in a death grip between her teeth. Her gaze met his for a brief second before her lashes lowered, concealing her emotions.

The urge to protect her, claim her like a goddamn caveman sprouted up stronger than ever. He stood and took a step toward her before he realized what he was doing. He stopped, shaking his head. It wasn't his place to comfort her. It was Mark's.

With regret, Tristan bypassed Sara and climbed the stairs to the second floor, in search of Shame. He needed to get the hell out of there. Get some air, before he did or said something he would regret. Shame would understand and take care of things for Tristan while he was gone.

༄༅༆

Sara tucked an exhausted Sam into bed and felt like weeping in relief when he drifted right off to sleep without the typical resistance he usually gave her at bedtime. That he didn't even put up a token fight against sleep showed her how worn out he was.

Sam had passed most of the afternoon by playing inside with either Shame or herself, sometimes both of them. Though Sara didn't want to like Tristan's partner, as they passed time together she found herself beginning to. He was surprisingly good with Sam and possessed a wicked sense of humor that made her laugh and blush more in one afternoon than she could remember doing in the last several years.

Somewhere around dusk Shame had excused himself, saying that he needed to go outside and set up the night watch. After that Sam's demeanor rapidly slid downhill. Sam begged to go outside with Shame. Sara said no, that he needed to stay inside with her. The word no signaled the beginning of an all-evening temper tantrum. He screamed and cried and carried on until she wished her hearing would fail. He wanted to go outside and play with his new friend Shame. He wanted to go outside and play with his dog. Bob the dog was still missing, so that wasn't an option. No matter what she suggested in replacement of those two forbidden activities, nothing else would suffice.

She blamed his poor attitude on the stressful environment around him. They all did their best to shield him from the worst of it, but he was a smart kid. The tension level in the house skyrocketed. Bad vibes were so thick in the air they were palpable. Obviously Sam was reacting to it. He was just confused about what was going on around him. She couldn't blame him, she didn't understand half of what was happening herself.

Her shoulders drooped as she walked down the hall to the bathroom. It felt like the weight of the world rested on them. Every single thing she'd thought she'd known about life had been blown to smithereens.

A serial killer, a damn vampire of all things, was out to get her. That something like vampires existed at all was hard enough to swallow. But it couldn't be that cut and dry for her. There would be no half measures for Sara McCoy. Everything had to be done the hard way. She had to be attacked, almost raped by a supernatural creature, somehow manage to survive it, and now contend with the knowledge that he was still out there thinking up new inventive ways to finish her off.

When she'd called in to work, requesting the following week off, her boss had been less than enthused. Of course, when she'd explained that she'd been attacked in the middle of the night—leaving out the bits that were unbelievable—Mr. Morgan had changed his tune. He went from tyrannical boss to nosy coworker in the blink of an eye. When he kept insisting he stop by to check on her, she'd finally had to snap at the man, telling him she was fine with the protection she had and disconnect before she said something she'd regret. Like where he could stick his journalistic curiosity. She was not going to be the next cover of his sad little paper. She could almost see the headline, "Woman attacked by monster and saved by ghost of dead lover".

Mark was right about it sounding a lot like a cheesy horror flick. She would have been amused, had it not been her life she was dealing with.

If that weren't enough, she also had two very pissed off men to contend with. Or maybe it was one pissed off man and one indifferent man. Who could tell? Tristan was impossible to read. The way he'd left without a word seemed like something a person would do if they were mad, but it was possible she was only seeing what she wanted to see. Chances were good that he'd left because he simply didn't give a damn.

Mark, on the other hand, was pissed off. As soon as Tristan had left, he'd calmed down some and seemed more like himself for a little while. Until Shame came downstairs and informed them he and Tristan would be spending the night, so they could watch over them. Mark blew a gasket at the suggestion of

Tristan sleeping over. She'd begrudgingly admitted to feeling more secure with them there and Mark hadn't liked that one little bit. She tried to make him understand her reasoning—that protecting Sam was of the utmost importance—but he'd refused to hear her out. After that they had fought about everything and nothing at all.

At the end of the argument he'd accused her of lusting after Tristan, of responding to his sexual advances. It didn't seem to matter that he had no basis for his accusation. Though he had no idea what had happened between her and Tristan earlier that morning, Sara did. And her contrary body refused to let her forget a single second of it. The guilt ate away at her, even while her body clamored for Tristan to finish what he'd started. That Tristan seemed unaffected by it all, enforced her anger.

Sara was so damn mad she couldn't think straight. Mark lashed out at her and she wasn't about to sit there and take it. She was determined to give back as good as she got.

When Mark accused her of fucking Tristan and Shame, Sara said the first thing that popped into her head. "So what?"

Mark's face turned red and a vein began to pulse in his forehead in response to her snide suggestion. Then she'd done the worst thing she could have, she laughed. Mark called her a two-timing whore and stormed out of the house before she could say another word. Instead of going after him like she should have, she sat, her ass glued to the seat cushion, while he peeled rubber backing out of the driveway.

When the loud roar of his engine couldn't be heard any longer, Sara buried her face in the couch arm and cried. She wept enough tears to fill the damn ocean for what a fool she was. Other than her son, Mark was the only soul she could count on in the world and she drove him away, just like everyone else.

The part of herself she hated—the needy, clingy part—screamed inside her head. On the outside, Sara dried her eyes and tried to pretend everything was okay.

Sara had calmly gone in search of her son. She found him and Shame playing a game of Monopoly and joined in. She smiled and joked at the appropriate intervals, right along with them, but her inner voice, the crybaby that it was, wouldn't shut up. It continued to rant and rave in her ears.

They weren't going to come back. Neither one of them. No one had ever stuck around for her before—not her father, who left her to follow his career; not her mother, who couldn't cope with being alone and had chosen to end her own life rather than stick around and raise her only daughter. Tristan himself had left her to pursue greener pastures. Why should she ever expect anything to end differently? Everyone she'd ever cared about had chosen to leave her. One way or another she always ended up alone. It looked as if she was destined to stay that way.

Arrrrghhh! It was a sad day when listening to your own whining made you sick. One sharp, mental bitch slap and the voice in her head quieted.

The house was quiet. Other than Sam, asleep down the hall, she was alone, with only her thoughts to keep her company.

Sara puttered around the bathroom, setting out the things she wanted for her bath. She turned on the radio, flipping it to her favorite oldies station, and adjusted the volume. She wanted to be able to hear it but she didn't want it to be so loud that it drew attention.

As far as she knew Shame was still standing guard somewhere outside. Knowing he was there, watching out for them, gave her a small measure of comfort.

Neither Tristan, nor Mark, had come back. They were probably off pouting somewhere together, comparing notes and talking about what a bitch she was. The thought of the two of them together, like old times, made her smile in spite of her worries.

Sara tested the water temperature with her toes, making sure it wasn't too hot before climbing in. A nice hot bath was her never-fail cure for a shitty day. Resting her head on the fluffy, pink, bath pillow, her eyelids fell shut.

Calgon, take me away...

She tried to concentrate on the feel of the gently scented water lapping against her skin, the soft music floating in the air around her, and found that she couldn't. Her never-fail cure was doing just that—failing. Go figure, when she needed it the most it wasn't going to be any help.

Her mind refused to stop spinning. A plethora of clipped thoughts and questions ran on a non-stop loop in her head. Her body was strung as tight as a guitar string, on the verge of snapping. Even the aromatherapy candles she lit, for the extra umph she thought they would bring, weren't working. The lavender scent smelled pleasant, but they definitely weren't making good on their promise to aide in relaxation. The box claimed your satisfaction was guaranteed or your money would be refunded.

Sara wanted her damn money back.

This was all Tristan's damn fault. All of her problems—the confusion and mixed emotions—could be laid right at his size-thirteen boots. Even the attack, as random as it seemed, could be traced back to him. Was it only a coincidence that the same man...thing...he was searching for targeted her as its next victim, or something else?

That one thought brought forth scads of others. Thoughts she'd been avoiding because of their potential to rip the scabs off old wounds and make her bleed anew. Regardless of the damage they could do, they forced their way into her head. One after another, they poured out of her subconscious, not giving her the chance to answer any of them.

Strangely enough the one thought that bothered her the most had nothing to do with the attack. Sara wondered, if none of the last twenty-four hours had taken place, would she have continued to live out the rest of her life believing that Tristan was dead and buried, never knowing the truth? Sara was fairly sure she already knew the answer.

There had to be something more peaceful she could think about. What was the cliché people on television said, something about finding your happy place? It was a good idea in theory. Unfortunately, all of her happy places involved at least one, if not both of the men turning her life upside down at the moment. She considered creating a new one, some random fantasy to make her forget about her problems for a little while.

Sara took a deep breath and put her imagination to work.

৪০৫৪

Tristan swaggered into a small pub not far from Sara's home and approached the bar. A petite blonde, who didn't look old enough to consume the drinks she served, sat behind the counter, a bored expression on her face. She noticed him and smiled, her emerald eyes lighting up, changing her appearance from average to pretty. "What can I get for you, handsome?"

"A beer. Whatever you have on draft." Tristan didn't smile back, hoping the girl would take the hint and know he wasn't interested, without him having to actually come out and say it.

He didn't want to hurt her feelings. While she went to fill him a glass, Tristan covertly scanned the room, looking for trouble, as had become habit. He was almost disappointed when he didn't find any. A fight would be just the thing he needed to rid himself of the extra energy raging through his system.

The bartender slid a frosted mug across the counter and he did the same with a ten dollar bill. "Keep the change," he mumbled before turning away, heading for the empty booth in the back.

He'd considered returning to Sara's after he'd left the apartment, but decided against it. With the black mood he was in, he wasn't good company for anyone. Being around Sara and Mark, the happy couple, he thought with a snort, would only light his fuse.

Tristan wanted her to be happy. He honestly did, but that didn't mean he wanted to have it shoved in his face. There was only so much one man could take.

When he'd left her place, he drove around for while, trying to calm down. It hadn't worked, but he hadn't really expected it to. He'd finally ended up back at the apartment, to sit and stew in his own juices. Once there, he'd remembered a transmission he and Shame had been scheduled for earlier and missed. Rushing to the computer, he'd hoped to head off his boss. Ramsey usually responded to a missed transmission by immediately hopping on a plane and confronting those who were suspiciously absent. If he showed up, there would be hell to pay, not just for him but for Shame as well and he didn't want his partner to suffer for helping him out.

He wasn't sure what he hoped to accomplish but he needn't have worried about it. When he logged in to the secure email service he was greeted by twelve messages, one from his boss and the other eleven spam. The email he'd worried about only said that their transmission had been cancelled, to be rescheduled at a later date. Apparently Ramsey had been called away due to a family emergency.

The words *family emergency* glared off the screen at him. After six years of working under the man, Tristan hadn't been aware the old goat had a family. It was ironic that the bastard responsible for taking away his and Shame's freedom was allowed to carry on a normal life, have a family, while the men under him were ripped away from theirs. Tristan punched the wall, the plaster crumbling under his fist, and enjoyed the sting to his knuckles. It was dumb and immature but it took the edge off his temper.

Kind of the same way he felt now. After three beers, Tristan still felt like shit. The alcohol wasn't doing its job at all. His thoughts were still chaotic and he couldn't rid himself of the burning jealousy he felt whenever he thought of Mark and Sara. He had to move past it. He needed to keep reminding himself why he was there. That he was supposed to protect Sara and Sam, catch the vampire before he harmed anyone else, and get the hell out of town…that was it. He wasn't there to rekindle old romances. Maybe, if he kept telling himself that, he would eventually start believing it.

Mark strolled into the bar, just as Tristan waved at the waitress for another drink. The man spotted him instantly and headed for him, a malevolent gleam in his eyes. He stopped short of the table, his fists swinging at his sides, and spoke, his voice loud, "What the hell are you doing here?"

What little mellow Tristan felt sped away, leaving him with nothing but his anger and Mark there to take it out on. If he'd been a lesser man he would've just beat the shit out of him and been done with it. Since he'd never been a man who took the easy way out, he didn't, though it was tempting. "Sit down, Mark. You're causing a scene," Tristan said.

Mark glanced behind him and noticed half the room staring their way curiously. With an exaggerated huff, he slid heavily into the booth seat across from Tristan, his eyes narrowed into angry slits. "I would've thought you'd be back at Sara's, busy fucking her raw."

Tristan gritted his teeth. It was one thing if Mark wanted to strike out at him. It was an entirely different matter when he brought up Sara. He wasn't about to sit there and listen to Mark badmouth her. Leaning forward over the table, he kept his voice deceptively calm. "I would watch my mouth, if I were you."

"That's right," Mark replied, his lips twisting into a cruel parody of a smile. "That's not your style anymore, is it? You're more of a knock 'em up and run type of—"

Tristan leapt over the table and pulled Mark up by the front of his shirt. "You shut your fucking mouth. You don't know anything about me or why I left."

"Get your damn hands off me," Mark sputtered.

"Let's, you and I, come to an understanding first. You can say what you will about me. I couldn't care less about your opinion, but you will not bring Sara into it. I won't stand by and listen to you malign her character. You get me?" Tristan tightened his grip when Mark didn't answer. "Are we clear?"

"Crystal," he finally answered, his tone belligerent. Wrapping his hands around Tristan's wrists, he jerked them off his shirt. Mark stayed right where he was, looking Tristan square in the eye. "For your information, my friend," he spat out sarcastically, "I wouldn't do anything to hurt Sara or Sam. You've done enough of that all by yourself."

Guilt swamped Tristan. Mark was right. He had hurt Sara and Sam, though not intentionally. He hadn't had a choice. Of course they didn't know that. They both thought he'd just left, faking his own death rather than sticking around. It had him tied up in knots that he couldn't tell them any differently.

He waved for the waitress to bring over a pitcher of beer, instead of the single mug he'd requested a moment before. Mark looked like he could use a drink, or ten, as bad as Tristan could. He wanted to get drunk and forget that the last week had happened at all. It would have been better for everyone involved if he'd never stepped foot back in town. If not for finding out about his son he would've wished he could erase the whole experience.

Both men sat, drinking one mug of cold beer after another. Silence stretched uncomfortably between them, hostile glares arrowing back and forth over the table.

Mark was the first to break the silence. "Why couldn't you just stay away?" He looked down into his beer as if the answer to his questions could be found there before glancing back up. "You left her pregnant and alone. Just when Sara was beginning to move on with her life...here you are, back to screw things up."

"I didn't know Sara was pregnant," Tristan admitted.

"Like that makes it okay. We thought you were dead. Hell, we even had a funeral. Sara insisted on it, even though there was no body to bury." The fluorescent light in the bar caught the moisture in Mark's eyes, making them sparkle.

Tristan gulped. He wasn't good with emotions. He never had been. "I didn't mean to hurt anyone." *You or Sara.*

"Well, a fat lot of good that does now. Sara agreed to marry me. Did you know that?"

Tristan's jaw tightened, popping under the pressure he exerted on it. When he spoke, it was through clenched teeth. "Yes."

"Really? So you thought, what? That you didn't want her but you didn't want anyone else to have her either?"

"No. I want Sara to be happy."

"She was, until you showed up. Now everything's different. I barely had a chance with her when she thought you were dead. Now that she knows differently there's no way she's going to go through with it. Not if there's even the slightest chance that she can have you."

"I don't want her." The lie rolled smoothly off Tristan's tongue.

"Yeah right. That's why you couldn't take your eyes off of her. Why you stared at her with so much lust in your eyes I was surprised you didn't both go up in flames."

"It doesn't matter what I want. I'm only here to do a job. As soon as it's done, I'm out of here."

"Yeah." Mark laughed, the sound hollow and acrimonious. "You'll be gone and I'll be left to pick up the pieces, just like always."

Tristan wanted to tell him to fuck off. He couldn't help being pissed off and jealous of the man who'd taken his place, but he also owed him a huge debt of gratitude for it. Mark had stuck around and taken care of Sara, and later Sam, while he hadn't been able to. There was nothing he could ever do to repay him for that.

"I don't want Sara. She's yours. So is Sam. The kid doesn't know who I am and I figure it would be for the best if he didn't find out. I'm leaving soon and it would only confuse him." Tristan's heart broke as he said the words that would clear the path for Mark. It was the best he could do to smooth over the disruption he'd caused in their lives. "It wasn't my intention to mess up things for the three of you. I'm sure you'll be very happy together." Tristan tipped back his mug and swallowed, letting the ice-cold beer wash away the bitter acid rising up his throat.

Mark looked at him as if he'd grown a second head. "You may not be here to screw things up, but you're doing a hell of a good job of it. It doesn't matter whether you want her or not. She thought you were dead for the last six years and she still wouldn't let herself move on. Now that she knows you're alive and out there somewhere, she'll never get past it. She won't let anyone in. I don't care what you say, what lies you sit there and try to tell me. I know there's still something between the two of you. Only an idiot would have missed the looks you shot at each other."

Mark shook his head and stood. "I'm leaving. Tell Sara that if she needs me, she knows where to find me." He pulled on his coat and turned to go. He spoke over his shoulder as he walked away. "You might be able to fool yourself, but you can't fool me, Tristan. You're still in love with her." He glanced back at Tristan. "Grab Sara and don't let her go this time. If you don't, I want you to know that I'll be there, ready to take her back. You won't get another chance with her."

Chapter Nine

Sara hurried to the front door, still dripping wet from her bath. Whoever was beating their fists against the door was going to get a mouthful when she got there. The knocking started up again just as she reached the door and yanked it open.

The angry words she was about to scream died in her throat. A police officer stood, his legs shoulder's width apart, his full lips turned down in a frown. His heavily muscled body, concealed beneath the dark blue uniform he wore, towered about her. He had to be at least six and a half feet to her paltry five foot even. For a moment, Sara was caught up in watching the intricate flex and play of those muscles before common sense intruded. "May I help you, officer?"

"Yes, ma'am," he replied, his voice a husky tenor. "I apologize for showing up so late, but I'm here collecting donations for the department's annual charity drive."

She gawked as he stepped around her and walked into the house, as if he'd been invited in. "It's rather late, Officer—" Sara squinted as she tried to read the name on his badge. She couldn't make out what it said, the letters too small for her to see without her contacts. "I'm not sure what I would be able to donate right now," she mumbled.

His gaze traveled up and down her body, taking in her state of dress, or undress, as she'd only taken the time to throw on a thin satin robe before running to see who was at the door. "Anything you want to give me would be most appreciated."

She watched his eyes fill with heat, and trembled. The authority he radiated intimidated her. It also turned her on. Her nipples peaked and rubbed against the silky material covering them. A rush of heat spread over her body when she saw that he had indeed noticed and was blatantly staring at her breasts.

His gaze finally climbed back up to her pink face and he winked at her. "Seems like those little ladies know exactly what they'd like to give."

It took Sara a moment before his words and the implication behind them sunk in. Her cheeks went up in flames. She should have been mad, but she wasn't. She was strangely excited by his attention.

She wanted to let the robe fall and give him what he was so openly suggesting. The only thing that stopped her was the chance that she'd misinterpreted his desires. Could someone be arrested for flashing a cop if they were in their own home when they did it?

She didn't think so. Her reservations dropped, right along with her robe. Naked and horny, she stood and let him look his fill. Judging by the bulge she saw extending along the pressed length of his pant leg, he liked what he saw. So did she.

Sara's hands crept slowly up her abdomen and lifted her breasts, offering them up to him. He accepted with a wicked smile, his hat and shirt coming off and hitting the floor. His belt, complete with gun, nightstick and a shiny pair of silver handcuffs remained at his waist.

Sara briefly wondered how many uses they could find for those last two items.

He came up against her, pressing her back into the banister behind her, and all thoughts fled. She moaned as the slats bit into the flesh of her back. His mouth covered one pink nipple and bit down on it. His grip loosened and the velvety flat of his tongue came out to lave over her swollen flesh. Sara's back arched in pleasure. She tried to shove her nipple back into his mouth, wanting more. He chuckled against her skin, the fan of his breath cool against her flushed skin. He denied her what she craved, continuing to leisurely lap at her, when what she wanted was the firm pressure of a moment before.

Her pussy throbbed and ached, clenching around the empty space she wanted his cock to fill.

Feeling wild and ravenous for the tool she felt pressing into her belly, Sara twined her arms around his neck and climbed him, her legs wrapping around his waist and holding on tight. She ground her crotch against him. The ridge of his cock rubbed in just the right place and made her body clench harder.

"You're a very naughty girl, aren't you?" he whispered into her ear.

"Yes," Sara said, going along with the game he wanted to play. "I've been very bad, Mr. Officer, I think I need to be taught a lesson. Maybe with the big nightstick you've got here." Sara's fingers wiggled into the space between their bodies and rubbed over his erection. "Mmm, and what a big nightstick it is."

He pulled back from her, setting her away from him, and looked down at her sternly. "I'll decide what your punishment should be, not you. Now turn around, lean forward and spread your legs."

His harsh order sent chills of anticipation down her spine. She did as he commanded. She wanted to be dominated and taken by this man. A man whose name she didn't even know.

The room was quiet behind her. All she could hear was the steady thump of her own heart beating heavily against her rib cage. Warm, rough hands came around her sides and started to rub down her body. Calloused fingertips invaded her, massaging through the sparse hair guarding her sex, and foraged further down into the wet folds beneath. His thumb pressed over her clit. His middle finger sank into her pussy and slowly thrust in and out, testing her readiness. Sara swallowed her demand for more and moaned. He was the one in charge now. She would have to trust that he would give her what she wanted.

"Very nice," he said. "I'm glad to see there aren't any concealed weapons on you. I would hate to have to take you in. The boys down at the station might like it though."

A little shiver went down her spine at the suggestion of being handcuffed naked and taken to the police station in the middle of the night. What would happen? Would they all laugh at her and poke fun? Or would they take turns using her any way they saw fit? A fresh rush of cream saturated her groin.

He noticed and plunged a second finger inside her. "I think you like that idea. You like the thought of being forced to service a bunch of horny police officers. Don't you?"

"Yes," Sara breathed. How could she deny it, when the evidence against her stained his fingers? "Just as a thought though." She whimpered when a third thick finger broke through her gate and forced its way into her cunt. "I wouldn't want to actually do it. I'm not like that."

"You're not like that? You seem like a pretty hot bitch to me."

Sara moaned as the rasp of a zipper being lowered sounded behind her. She thrust her hips back, anxious for him to fuck her.

He slapped her on the ass. "Impatient one, aren't you?"

His cupped palm struck one tender cheek and then the other, switching sides on every impact. Waves of pure sensation crashed over her with each smack. She was going to come. The tension inside her coiled and tightened until she thought she was going to pass out from the pleasure/pain of it.

He stopped when she was right on the brink of orgasm and swung her around, hauled her off her feet and over his shoulder. He carried her that way, like a sack of potatoes, up the stairs. She admired his tight ass, bouncing against him with every step. Unable to resist, she reached down and pinched it hard between her thumb and forefinger.

He cursed and quickened his pace. Entering her bedroom, he went straight to the bed and dumped her off on it. Sara fell on her back and stared up at him, trying to convey how badly she wanted him with the look on her face.

He dropped to his knees and buried his face between her thighs, his tongue burrowing into the soft, wet center he found there. He rimmed the opening to her vagina with a firm tongue, making her mewl, before forcing it inside her. He fucked in and out of her with his tongue until Sara was nothing more than a mindless, writhing mass of horny nerves.

"Please," Sara said. "Please, do it. Make me come."

He halted. The delicious sensations coursing through her came to an abrupt end. The building orgasm shriveled to barely perceivable ripples of unfulfilled longing. She glanced down, looking through her bent knees, to see what the problem was.

And it was a big problem that met her stunned gaze. The cop wasn't there. In his place was Tristan, staring back at her, his vivid blue eyes full of wicked merriment.

Sara opened her eyes and stared at the white-tiled bathroom around her. Her fantasy ruined, she slapped the water in frustration. Leave it to Tristan to creep into her thoughts and even somehow manage to ruin her alone time. Damn him.

By the time Tristan sobered up enough to drive it was late, not quite eleven. Shame had been on guard at Sara's for the better part of the day and needed to be relieved. Tristan figured he would take the late shifts from that night on. If he was outside, in the cold night air, maybe his ardor would diminish along with the temperature. He could only resist so much temptation. Just the thought of her lying warm and practically naked, between crisp sheets, was enough to make him sweat.

Tristan parked a block away from Sara's house and hoofed the rest of the way on foot. He didn't want to draw attention to his and Shame's presence by parking outside her house. Halfway through the backyard, he ran into Shame. His partner's eyes widened when he noticed Tristan, as if he hadn't expect to see him so soon. "Hey, bro, can't say I'm not glad to see you. I think my balls are frozen to my legs, it's so cold out here."

Tristan chuckled. "You're in an awfully good mood tonight. What have you been up to while I was gone?"

"Well," Shame drawled, "I have to admit that's a pretty great kid you've got there. I spent most of the day playing games with him, just keeping him occupied mostly. Sara joined us after she got in a big round with her old man. What was his name again?"

"Mark."

"Yeah—Mark. So anyway, Sara joined us after he took off. I didn't get to spend a whole lot of time with her though. Thanks to those damn clouds it got dark earlier than usual tonight and I had to come out here."

"So?" Tristan asked.

"So what?"

"So what did you think?"

Shame smiled. "Of Sara?"

"Yes, Sara. Are you going to make me spell it out for you?"

Shame chortled. "No, I'm not that mean. Like I said, man, I didn't get the chance to spend much time with her, but I can see the attraction. She's one hot cookie. So hot, in fact, that I wouldn't mind having a go at her myself."

Tristan bristled at his friend's comment. Shame saw it and laughed harder. "Hey, man, I was just saying is all. I'm not going to make a move on her. I swear."

"Mm-hmm," Tristan mumbled.

"I won't. If you were smart, you'd be up there with her right now, instead of standing out here with me. That dude—Mark—hasn't come back yet."

"I know that already. I ran into him when I stopped to have a few cold ones before coming back here."

"Well, I don't see any bruises," he said, looking Tristan over. "So, you must have beat his ass before he threw the first punch, eh?"

"Nope. I bought him a drink or three and we had a little talk."

Shame winced. "Brutal. Personally, I'd have rather taken the ass-beating."

"It wasn't that bad. He did say he wouldn't come back until we were gone though."

"Sweet," Shame replied. "That takes care of that obstacle. I'd say that pretty much paves the way right into Sara's panties for you."

"Not going to happen, my friend. I do have some self-control."

Shame's smile grew wicked. "So if I told you she was upstairs right now, naked and wet, waiting for you, you'd pass?"

Tristan snorted. "I said I had self-control, not that I was dead from the waist down."

"Glad to hear that. I was starting to worry about you. I know I'm irresistible, but we both know you need to get laid—by a woman. You know what they say, sometimes you want a nut and sometimes you don't." Shame laughed at his own lame humor and thumped Tristan on the back.

"You're not right, man," Tristan said. "I think you have a few screws loose upstairs."

"No, I'm all there. You're just jealous 'cause my dicks bigger than yours is."

"Jesus, you're crazy. Only in your dreams is your cock bigger than mine. Now drop it. We have more important things to discuss."

They stood outside and talked about their missed transmission and various other things, until Shame yawned and Tristan told him to go on in the house and get some sleep. Finally, Tristan was alone, with only his chaotic thoughts to keep him company.

He walked the perimeter of the house and yard, trying to keep warm. He'd only made a few passes when Shame came back outside.

"Tristan," he shouted. "I need for you to get in here. I think there's something wrong with Sara."

Tristan's heart jumped into his throat and lodged there as he ran across the yard. He passed Shame, vaguely hearing him say the word bathroom. Tristan didn't take the time to stop and find out. He raced up the stairs two steps at a time, his pulse thundering in his ears.

He reached the bathroom a breath after Shame yelled for him. He yanked at the knob. Locked. Tristan took a few steps back, braced himself and kicked the door in.

ಬಂಡ

Sara lay in the bathtub, on fire for the orgasm that had been so close to fruition, but was now about as substantial as ashes in the wind. Her fantasy had been perfect. The very thing to help get her off. Or it would have been, had Tristan not invaded it.

Damn him! First he left her in need that morning. Now she couldn't even masturbate without him popping into her mind, taunting her with what she couldn't have. The man was going to be the death of her.

Sara sighed in frustration. She might as well give it up. It wasn't going to happen. Her body was strung tight, in need of a fix, but her mind wasn't going to cooperate. That much was apparent.

The bath water had long since gone tepid around her. Her body was starting to prune up like a raisin. It was past time to get out.

Sara blew out the candles around her and grabbed hold of the cool, ceramic lip of the tub for balance. She rose up out of the water and reached for a towel. The doorknob rattled and burst open, shreds of wood flying inward. She shrieked, jumping back, her arms flailing wildly for purchase as she felt herself slipping.

Tristan forced his way into the room just in time to catch Sara's wet, slippery, naked body in his arms. It took a few deep breaths before his anger overcame his worry. There wasn't anything wrong with Sara. Shame was just being his usual pain-in-the-ass self. When Tristan got his hands on Shame, he was going to kill him.

For now though, he planned to give all his thought to the wiggling bundle of wet woman in his arms. He tightened his hold around Sara's waist and pulled her closer. One finger tipped her chin up so he could look her in the eye. "What the hell are you trying to do, give me a heart attack?"

He felt her stiffen and cursed under his breath. Why couldn't he keep his big mouth shut? He couldn't ever seem to do the right thing around her.

Her eyes flared wide as she squirmed against him, trying to get away. He smothered a groan when her hand inadvertently grazed his crotch. His cock roared to life. His jeans suddenly felt two sizes too small. All he wanted was to lower her onto the floor, and thrust into her soft, pliant body.

Sara pulled back, her nose scrunching up at him. "The last I checked, what I do or don't do is none of your concern anymore. You lost the privilege to stick your nose in my business a long time ago. Right about the time you decided to fake your own damn death."

"I'll show you what privileges I'm entitled to." Tristan swung her up, one arm around her legs, the other around her chest, pinning her arms to her sides.

"Put me down!" Sara twisted in his arms, her middle rising and falling like a bronc trying to buck a rider.

"Quit squirming, I'm not going to let you go."

"Funny, I remember you saying something along those lines when we were together. It didn't take very much for you to change your mind and walk away then."

Tristan ignored Sara's feeble attempts to get away from him. "I'm not going to let you go," he repeated stiffly. "Not until we get a few things straight between us."

"There is nothing I need to get straight with you. Just leave me alone."

"No."

Sara didn't say anything else. He got to briefly enjoy the sensation having her in his arms. Her weight felt good there, like it belonged. His reprieve ended as soon as he stepped over the threshold of her bedroom. Sara went crazy, struggling and trying to bite him.

His gaze quickly took in the room as he tried to hang onto her. Light-wood furniture dominated it. A bed, two dressers, a vanity. The frilly mauve curtains and bedspread were toned down by warm shades of blue in the pillows that lay atop the bed.

"Will you calm down? I'm not going to do anything you don't want me to do."

"So you're going to sit me down and leave?"

"You don't really mean that, Sara."

"I do mean it. Nothing would make me happier than for you to disappear as fast as you resurfaced."

That she wouldn't look him in the eyes told him everything he needed to know. She was lying.

"Well I guess you've made a liar out me, because I'm not going anywhere." He dropped her on the bed, stood back, his arms crossed over his chest, and admired the naked length of her.

Sara was spread across the bed, her body more tempting than a feast lying before a starving man. Her chest rose and fell with each inhalation, pushing her breasts up and out and drawing his gaze to the firm thrust of them. Her ribs narrowed down to a slim waist, one his hand itched to span. The gentle curve of her generous hips flared below. Her thighs were squeezed closed, hiding her sex from him, making him want to separate her legs, lap at the sweet cream she would release for him.

Tristan shuddered. His cock leapt in excitement.

She was a work of art. All soft curves on top of lean muscle. Her breasts and hips were slightly fuller than before, but they only added to her appeal, made him want her more.

An image of what she must have looked like, her body rounded with his child, popped into his mind and lodged there. The picture increased his need for her. He wanted to lose himself inside her warmth, wallow in it and forget all the time, the hurt that loomed like a white elephant between them.

Tristan pulled his shirt over his head and let it fall to the floor. His gaze met hers as he worked the buttons on his jeans and kicked out of them. Since he hadn't taken the time to put on boxers when they were interrupted, he was left naked and vulnerable before her. His cock jutted out of the dark thatch at its base, balls heavy and swollen beneath.

Sara's eyes warmed. He felt her reaction like an intimate caress. Her eyelids lowered as she shyly took in his form. When her perusal stopped at the junction of his legs, her pink tongue darted out, moistening her bottom lip. Tristan groaned. It was all too easy to imagine her mouth on him, like it was earlier that morning, before they were interrupted. His erection bobbed up another inch, grazing the flesh below his navel, showing off, longing for her loving touch as much as he did.

Tristan propped one knee on the bed. Sara's expression went from eager to apprehensive. Scooting to the farthest corner of the mattress, she eyed him nervously. "Tristan, I don't think this is such a good idea."

"Best idea I've had in years," Tristan murmured.

He moved toward her, grabbed one slender ankle and tugged her back across the bed. She lay rigid beside him. He settled on his side, one arm propped under his head. "Loosen up, Sara. I'm not going to hurt you. You know that."

Fire blazed behind her eyes. "How am I supposed to know that? I don't know anything about you anymore. Don't have any idea what you're capable of."

It stung that she doubted him, but he couldn't really blame her. He would just have to prove himself to her and re-earn her trust. Bending forward, he traced the shell of her ear with his tongue. "You know me, Sara. I'm the same man you used to love." His palm swept over her arm, felt the goose bumps that appeared in the wake of his touch.

"Let me make love to you, Sara. You don't know how many nights I've lain awake dreaming of you, of tasting your sweet pussy, making love with you, like we used to."

Sara shivered. Her eyes met his and she searched his gaze, looking for something. She must've seen what she wanted because a second later she nodded her acceptance. Tristan sighed in relief. She wasn't going to turn him away. For a moment there, he'd been worried she would do exactly that. He wanted her. Bad enough to coerce her into seeing things his way, but not enough to make her do something she didn't want.

Sara licked her lips. Tristan avidly watched the slow progression of her tongue over the expanse of mouth, her plump bottom lip beckoning him. Happy to oblige, he sucked the moist offering into his mouth, nipping it with his teeth. Sara inhaled sharply.

His tongue quickly soothed the hurt away. Her mouth parted in response and Tristan took advantage, slipping his tongue inside to rub sinuously over her hers. She tasted sweet, like fresh raspberries and bottled sex.

Sara moaned and he deepened the kiss, thrusting his tongue in and out, alongside hers, in mimic of making love. She wiggled, the diamond-hard tips of her breasts digging into his chest. His control was shot. It had been so long...he needed her so much...

He pushed Sara to her back and followed her down, their mouths fused together. A sexy little squeak issued from between her lips as he sipped from her. He wanted to pull more of those sexy noises out of her, make her moan in pleasure. Scream his name as she came in his mouth.

Tristan left the sweet haven of her mouth and worked his way down her neck to her shoulder. He paused as he reached her breasts, admiring her luscious curves. "Damn, baby, you have the prettiest little tits," he whispered huskily. "I think I'm going to have to spend a lot of time right here, sucking on your sweet nipples."

"I like the way your mind works." Sara moaned as he took the tip of her breast into his mouth. He sucked and laved each nipple, over and over, taking turns with each until they stuck out, red and wet, from his attention.

He ran wet kisses from her clavicle to her bellybutton and dipped his tongue inside, his ego soaring when she groaned and arched her hips up against his touch. He hadn't forgotten that her bellybutton was one of her hot spots. He remembered everything that made her howl.

Tristan worked his way down her stomach, enjoying the soft texture to her skin, the smell of it. He licked and nipped at her gently as he went along. Reaching the apex of her sex, he breathed in deeply. God, there was nothing like the smell of her, his woman. The scent of her hot, aroused body filled him. Musk and honey. He wanted nothing more than to devour her. Eat her until she passed out from the pleasure only he could give her.

His tongue extended, swiping lazily through her slit, tasting the sweet cream of her essence. He groaned as the pungent flavor of her desire swept over his taste buds. "God, you taste so damn good, Sara."

Sara moaned and arched her hips. He buried his tongue deeper, making long laps through the swollen folds of her sex. He homed in on the tiny kernel of nerves at her center and focused his attention there, gliding his tongue over and around it, milking it with his lips.

Sara's fingers threaded through his hair, holding him where he was. "Yes. Harder! Oh God."

Tristan could have told her he wasn't going anywhere, but he knew better than to talk with his mouth full. As it was, he could barely breathe. She was all around him, her pussy wet and clinging, her sweet voice crying out for more of the delicious torment he wanted to drag on forever.

Two fingers rose up to join in. He speared one, then the other into her while she mewled, begging for more. The tight walls of her sex gripped his fingers like a vise, drawing him in and clamping down, fighting him as he plunged them in and out.

The walls of Sara's pussy began to ripple, sucking his fingers in deeper. "That's it, Sara. Come for me, baby." He doubled his efforts, licking harder, fucking her faster with his fingers.

Sara came with a long groan, his name on her lips, her thighs trembling around his head.

Flicking his tongue over her fiery red clit once more, Tristan pulled back to admire his handiwork. Sara lay satisfied on the bed, her arms flung above her head, legs splayed wide open. The corners of her lips were turned up, her smile adorable in its serenity.

"You aren't going to sleep on me, are you?"

Sara's eyelids lifted a fraction, her smile widening. "Come here," she said, her fingers moving in a come-hither motion. "It's my turn. Bring that sexy body of yours up here." She licked her lips. "Fuck my mouth."

"As tempting as that sounds, I'm going to pass," he growled.

Sara's eyes widened. She sucked her bottom lip into her mouth and chewed on it for a second before speaking. "Are...are you leaving?" Her voice broke on the last word, shattering his heart.

"I'm not going anywhere. I want to make love with you. I meant I didn't want any more foreplay. Just being near you is enough to drive me crazy. I need to be inside you, princess."

She held her arms out for him and he willingly fell into them, wrapping her in his arms and holding her close. Their hips lined up, his cock nudging her center, and he pressed down, feeding the length of his shaft into the heart of her inch by inch until he felt the smooth skin of her ass kiss his balls.

Her pussy clasped around his length, bathing it in hot, wet heat. Tristan groaned, the sense of coming home complete. This was where he belonged, with this woman he loved more than life itself.

He pumped his hips, slow and lazy, his gaze riveted on his cock as it forged in and out of her tight heat, her cream glistening on his shaft. Sara's light moans and whimpers peppered the air, along with the wet sucking noises her body made on his every retreat. It was a damn erotic sight. His balls agreed, tightening and hugging the base of his cock. Tristan reached down and jerked on them, forcing his orgasm back. He didn't want to come. He wanted to make this time with her last.

"Harder, damn it," she begged, moaning and squirming beneath him. Her hands gripped his ass and pulled him deeper into her. He growled and gave in to her demands. Fucking her harder and faster. His cock slamming into her over and over again.

All too soon he felt the walls of her cunt collapse and convulse around the shaft of his cock. Sara shrieked, screaming his name. It was too much. It felt too damn good. He let himself go, let her release carry him away with her. His body tensed, shaking with the power of his orgasm. He held onto her tightly, let her be his anchor, as he emptied himself inside her, the contractions so powerful his vision blurred, reality outside of their joined bodies ceasing to exist.

His body went limp, drained from the agonizing pleasure of his orgasm. Tristan felt Sara shift beneath him. He had to be crushing her. He rolled to his back and took her with him, not willing to be separated from her.

Chapter Ten

Sara curled into Tristan's warmth. Her head rested on his shoulder, one leg draped across his. Her fingers toyed absentmindedly through the silky dark hair between his pecs. Damn, it felt so good to be in his arms again.

Tristan moaned in his sleep, his forehead wrinkled as if he were dreaming. From the expressions he made, it wasn't a pleasant one. She could relate.

Oddly enough, she'd fallen fast asleep in his arms, right after he gave her the best two orgasms of her life, dream-free for the first time in weeks. It didn't seem fair that he could slay the bad guys both in real life and her subconscious. The man was too much.

Sara lifted the sheet, glancing down at his semi-erect penis. Yep, he was too much all right. Her mouth watered. Would it be too naughty to sneak down under the covers and take a little taste? No, she decided. He'd had his turn at her, now it was her chance to play.

Sara slid beneath the comforter until she was face to genitals with him. Her breath blew over him and his cock twitched in response. Out of spite she did it again and was instantly rewarded with another twitch.

For some reason that tickled her funny bone. She swallowed down a giggle. She couldn't take the chance on waking him up before she started her intimate revenge. He would stop her, like he had earlier, and she really wanted to take him this way, to make love to him with her hands, her mouth. Sara flicked her tongue out, drawn to the tight ridge bisecting his balls, and licked him. He moaned in his sleep, shifting. Sara froze until it sounded like his breathing had evened back out. She did it again. This time she wanted to groan at the delicious taste of him. She could easily get addicted to his salty-sweet flavor.

With the next lick she continued on up, past his balls, the flat of her tongue moving over the length of his shaft. Her mouth poised over the ruby head of his erection, she was ready to suck him in when rough hands grabbed her under her arms and dragged her out from underneath the covers.

The damage was done though. She'd seen it. Now she understood why he'd put the blindfold on her. What she didn't understand was what the small tattoo just under the crown of his penis—TO1—meant.

Tristan pulled her out from underneath the covers, a frown between his eyes. The pissed-off look on his face confused her. Wouldn't most guys love to be woken up with a blow job?

"Want to tell me what you were doing down there?"

"Well," she drawled, trying to make a joke out of it. "If I have to explain it to you then I must not have been doing it right."

"You saw, didn't you?"

"Saw what?" If he felt that bad about her seeing his stupid tattoo, she would just pretend she hadn't noticed it. It was so tiny, it would be easy to miss anyway.

Tristan didn't buy her act. He turned away from her, but not before she caught the way his face flushed, as if he were embarrassed. It was a strange way for him to react.

"What does it mean?"

His head snapped back, his eyes meeting hers. "It's not important," he stated flatly. His tone told her the exact opposite. Whatever the damn thing meant, it was important, otherwise why would he make such a big deal about her seeing it? That he didn't want to share its meaning with her hurt more than she cared to admit even to herself.

"Fine," Sara snapped. She got up and walked over to the dresser. If he didn't want to share anything with her besides his overgrown penis, then that was fine by her. She didn't give a damn.

Her nose burned, calling her a liar. Tears filled her eyes. Sara dug through the drawers, her back to Tristan. She would be damned before she let him know he'd hurt her. In fact, she'd be damned if she shed any more tears over the bastard at all. He'd been the cause of enough of them already.

Sara yanked a nightshirt over her head, not caring what she pulled on as long as she was covered. Being naked in his presence suddenly made her feel dirty, used. She wiped off her tear-streaked face before turning back to him. He'd followed her example and put his clothes back on. He was getting ready to leave. Good. She was glad to be rid of him. Which didn't explain why the pain in her chest intensified.

Tristan looked at her hard. "You kept it?"

Sara wondered what the hell he was talking about until he nodded at her chest. In her haste to put something on, she'd grabbed the one article of clothing she shouldn't have, one of his old college jerseys. She felt heat crawling up her neck and spreading out over her cheeks. What a sentimental fool she must look like. She'd spent the last six years grieving for him, cleaving to his memory and raising their son. He must be getting a real kick out of seeing how pathetic she'd let herself become. Sara's back stiffened. Hell would freeze over before she answered his question. He could think what he wanted. Pride might not keep her warm at night but it was better than nothing. Right then it was the only thing keeping her from shattering into a million pieces upon the plush carpet under her feet.

"So you're leaving then?" she asked, careful to make her voice sound bored and uninterested.

"I need to give Shame a break," he said over his shoulder, already heading for the door.

Sara sank onto the bed, watching him. "Well thanks for the fuck. You were pretty good, but I'm sure Mark will be back soon. I won't need you to stand in for him again." The vengeful bitch in Sara's head cheered. She knew her spiteful words wouldn't hurt him much, it wasn't as if he cared about her, but they made her feel better.

Tristan's spine shot ramrod straight, like he was actually affected by what she'd said. She felt a twinge of remorse, but quickly hushed it. She was interpreting his actions into what she wanted them to mean. She knew he didn't give a shit about her.

He turned back, his face stained an angry red. Score one for Sara. She may not have been able to touch his shriveled-up, black heart but it looked like she'd scored a direct hit to his precious male ego.

"If this is the kind of bitch you've turned into, then I'm glad I didn't stick around to see it."

Sara sat and numbly watched him go. She fell to the bed as soon as the door closed behind him and buried her face in the pillow. Though her heart ached, a hollow emptiness expanding to vast proportions inside her chest, she was true to her word. Not a single tear was shed.

಄ఇ

Some time later, Sara woke. Someone was creeping around in her room. She sprang up, ready to scream for all she was worth, terrified that the vampire had come for her.

"Calm down, little lady. It's only me, Shame. I just wanted to check up on you."

The galloping in Sara's chest slowed to a mild canter. She flipped on the bedside lamp, allowing a weak glow to fill the room and illuminate her unexpected visitor. "How about you knock next time. You scared the crap out of me."

Shame smiled. "I only wanted to make sure you were okay." His smile grew wicked. "And maybe see if you slept in the buff."

Sara threw a pillow at him, laughing. The man was a character.

"You can't blame a guy for trying." He winked at her, sitting on the side of the bed. His face grew serious, making her wonder what he was thinking. "So what are you doing up here, all by your lonesome?"

Sara shrugged, not knowing what to say.

"I expected Tristan to spend the night up here with you. Imagine my surprise when he came storming out of the house, all surly like a bear, and ordered me to come in here with you and the kid."

Sara looked at him blankly. If he was fishing for information, he wasn't going to get it from her.

"Don't know what to say, huh? Yeah, well that makes two of us. We both know that man could go all night if he wanted to. I figured that's what he'd be doing with you tonight."

Sara bristled. The last thing she wanted to hear about was all the women Tristan had fucked over the years. No matter how strong she wanted to be, she could only take so much. Hearing all the gory details of Tristan's sexual conquests would be the last straw.

"Don't go all rigid on me," Shame said from beside her, yanking her out of her musings. "You know he hasn't been with a woman since you."

"Excuse me? If he hasn't been fucking his way through America then how would you know..." Sara's voice faded away as she added everything up in her head. "Oh," she said, his comment making things clear. "*Oh.*"

Shame looked at her curiously. "He didn't tell you, did he?"

"No," she answered softly. Tristan didn't want to tell her anything.

"Damn. Me and my big mouth. Tristan's going to kill me."

Her mind worked in circles. "Don't worry about it, I won't say anything."

Sara saw his jaw loosen in relief that she wouldn't let on that he'd said anything about his and Tristan's relationship. The next thing she saw was darkness. Her vision blurred and went black, as if she'd been dropped into a bottomless void. Scared, she reached out and latched onto the first thing she could find. Shame's shirt. "I can't see!" she exclaimed wildly. "Why the hell can't I see?"

Shame pulled her into his arms and sat her on his lap. Sara felt the firm muscles of his thighs flex under her bottom, smelled the woodsy scent of his aftershave, but couldn't see a damn thing.

She blinked rapidly, trying to understand what was happening to her. The rational part of her mind, the part she desperately clung to, was aware of where she was, safe at home, in her bedroom. Her sight began to tell her something completely different. Her bedroom with its soft pastels and comforting ambiance was not what she saw.

The vision Tristan warned her about came into focus... The darkness shifted and morphed into a lonely parking lot. A few random cars were scattered throughout, each one several spaces from the other. She heard heavy breathing that wasn't her own.

A young woman exited a dark building to her left and started across the parking lot. Sara could hear the sharp click of her heels tapping against the pavement. The woman came closer, walking directly toward Sara. Right toward where the predator stood watching, waiting to make his move. Upon closer inspection, Sara guessed the girl was in her early twenties. Though young, time hadn't been kind to her. Her tired and worn features screamed of a life filled with hard knocks. Dark, puffy circles rimmed her eyes. Her reed-slim body would cause most to think she worked to keep it that way, but paired with her sunken cheeks, it gave Sara the impression that it had been a while since her last good meal. The downward tilt to her shoulders put Sara in mind of an abused animal. Her heart went out to the poor girl.

Then she remembered why she was there. Why she was seeing any of this at all. Sara saw through the eyes of a killer, a vampire. The young woman was the vampire's next victim.

Sara screamed. She shouted for the girl to run. To hide. It was no use. No one could hear her.

The scene played on, like a bad movie Sara couldn't turn off. She was forced to watch as the monster moved stealthily through the shadows, getting closer and closer, preparing to strike, to kill.

Sara watched as the girl tried to unlock her car, her fingers unsteady as she fumbled with the keys. They fell out of her hand, rattling loudly as they hit the ground. She bent down for them and Sara knew what was coming. She tried to close her eyes, block it out, but couldn't.

The girl looked up, her eyes wild and scared. Sara stared into the dark orbs and felt like she was drowning in them. The vampire struck. A clawed hand slashed out, separating skin and muscle from bone. The girl's slender throat parted, blood gushing from the wound.

Sara screamed in horror and blissfully saw no more.

When next she opened her eyes she was back in her own body. Shame's face loomed inches from hers, his expression one of concern. She still sat on his lap, her thighs draped to one side of his. She squirmed, uncomfortable being so close to him, and instantly regretted it. His cock woke, growing long and hard under her bottom.

"Sorry, darling," Shame drawled. "He has a mind of his own."

His arms fell to his sides, releasing her. Sara jumped off his lap but remained within touching distance, her knees pulled beneath her chin, arms around her calves.

"Are you okay?" he asked.

"Just peachy," she replied shortly. "I see people being slashed to bits every day. No big deal." Sara laughed hysterically, her guffaws turning to great racking sobs.

Shame put his arms around her and held her while she tried to gain control over herself. Eventually her respiration evened out. Sara slumped against his side, her head resting companionably on his shoulder.

"We're going to need to talk about it, ask you some questions about what you saw. Do you think you'll be okay for that?"

"Yeah," she whispered, gulping in a lungful of air. "I'll be okay. If I could just have a minute..." Her voice wavered. "I just need a minute to collect myself."

"All right, you take your time. I need to go get Tristan anyway. He'll want to be here when we go through what you saw."

A case of nerves hit Sara. "No. Wait! I'll go with you. I need to look in on Sam anyway."

Shame's warm eyes filled with sympathy as they met hers, like he understood, knew that she didn't want to be alone. "Sure. I'll just wait outside in the hall while you put on some clothes. It's cold out."

Sara tugged on a pair of pajama bottoms and her bunny slippers. It wasn't a fashion statement but she was warm and that was all she cared about. Shame stood out in the hall, one hip propped against the wall, waiting for her like he promised. As shaky as she felt, Sara was grateful for his presence. She went to him and threw her arms around his waist, hugging him tightly before quickly letting go. "Thank you," she whispered.

"You're welcome," he replied, something that sounded like awe in his voice. Sara wondered at that. Had no one ever hugged the man before?

Side by side they walked down the hall. Sara stopped in front of her son's room. She started to turn the knob, only then noticing it was ajar. Trepidation filled her, causing her heart to gallop. She knew she'd shut it firmly behind her when she tucked him in. Sara flung the door open.

Tristan sat on the side of the bed, speaking in hushed tones to their sleeping son. He spared her a glance and then continued with what he was doing. Sara couldn't hear what he said but the gesture alone touched her as nothing else could. She watched, not wanting to interrupt, as Tristan smoothed a stray lock of black hair away from their child's face, his fingers lingering over the curve of his cheek.

Shame wasn't so concerned about intruding. He walked into the room and straight over to Tristan. "Hey, dude," he whispered. "Sorry to bother you, but Sara had her first vision. Thought you'd want to know."

Tristan looked up, right at Sara, his turbulent eyes locking with hers. A flush crept over his chiseled face, like he'd been caught with his pants down instead of spending time with their son. "Yeah."

Sara lowered her eyes and turned away. Shame joined her, both of them giving Tristan a moment alone with Sam. It wasn't long before he came out. She looked from one man to the other, uncomfortable standing between them. "Let's get this over with."

Chapter Eleven

Tristan was in hell. It had been two days since Sara's vision. They'd garnered exactly zip in the way of new information from the crime scene of the latest murder she'd vicariously witnessed. Nothing had happened since. No new murders, no clues to go on...absolutely nothing. He and Shame were at loose ends. They'd given up the outdoor patrols, both of them agreeing that they could keep just as good an eye on things while indoors. Tristan had long since come to regret that decision.

He and Sara perfected the art of coexisting without having anything to do with each other. When he saw her coming, he went the other way. She did the same thing. Messages were passed back and forth through Shame. It was juvenile, but effective. Shame wasn't so keen on it. He repeatedly threatened to throttle Tristan if they kept it up.

The one ray of sunshine in his otherwise gloomy existence was Sam. Although Sara hadn't told the boy who Tristan was, Sam was beginning to warm up to him. It wasn't the easy camaraderie Sam shared with Shame, but it was a start.

The morning after he and Sara made love, Sam had waltzed right up to him and started talking, like they were old buddies. Tristan had been taken aback by the easy acceptance. He wasn't sure who the kid got that from, but it wasn't him. Tristan had always been a tad standoffish with strangers. Leery of them.

Tristan walked into Sara's bedroom and picked up the phone on her nightstand, intending to order something to eat. He was starving. The only thing Sara kept in the house was health food that tasted like sawdust. He'd rather chew on his own arm than eat any more of that crap. It was a wonder Sam didn't waste away to nothing with the way she fed him.

Pizza sounded good, and he figured he could find one that delivered so they wouldn't have to leave the house. He hit the call button, ready to dial information and request a number for the closest one, when he realized someone was already on the other end of the line. The phone was ringing. He was about to put the phone down and give her some privacy, when Mark picked up on the other end. Tristan's good intentions went out the window.

"Mark?" Sara said uncertainly.

"Yeah. What do you want, Sara? I'm kind of busy here."

"Well, I um...I was wondering why you hadn't been by the last couple of days? That's not like you."

"I've been busy."

"Too busy to pick up the phone and let me know you're still alive? I was worried about you."

"I'm sorry you were worried. I'm fine."

"Um, okay."

"How are you and Sam?"

"Fine. Things are stressful here but we're fine. Sam misses you."

"But you don't, huh?"

"I didn't say that, Mark."

"Whatever. I have to go."

"Mark, wait!"

The dial tone rang in Tristan's ear. He set the receiver back in its cradle. The jackass hung up on her. Childishly, he was glad Mark was acting like such a prick. The other, more grownup part of him cringed for Sara. Tristan felt bad for her. Not *that* bad though. Mark apparently meant to stand by his word regarding staying away from Sara until Tristan was gone. She was better off without Mark hovering around her day and night anyway. He would be safer away from the house. Not that that was the only reason he was glad his former friend was no longer there. Mark wasn't the right man for her. She needed someone like him, someone who could take care of her and Sam, the way he could.

No, not someone like you. They need you, the contrary devil on his shoulder whispered in his ear.

"Shut up," he said aloud.

"I haven't even said anything yet," Shame replied, entering the room.

Tristan looked up as Shame made himself at home, plopping down on the bed like it belonged to him. He scowled. "The way I figure it, you're about due to give me another lecture. If that's the case, Shame, you can save it. You're wasting your breath."

"It's mine to waste and what better cause am I gonna find than trying to reunite two of the most stubborn, obstinate people I've ever had the pleasure to spend time with. I swear you were made for each other. You're both so deep in the river of denial that you need a damn paddle."

Tristan chose to ignore the last part. "You're one to talk. You're more hardheaded than I am."

"Not so, man. If I had a chance, no matter how short, to be with my family, I would make the most of it. You wouldn't find me moping around feeling sorry for myself like you're doing."

"Fuck you, Shame."

☼☾

Sara trudged up the stairs, a laundry basket filled with clean clothes in her arms. The phone call to Mark replayed in her head. She'd tried to call Cindy as well, only to get her voice mail. Again. While it wasn't unheard of for her ditzy friend to forget to turn on her cell, it was unlike her not to check her messages and return calls. Sara had been trying to reach Cindy since the morning after her attack, with no luck. Sara stopped at the entrance into her bedroom. Tristan and Shame sat on her bed, lost in conversation. Shame's arm was carelessly strung over Tristan's broad shoulders. Something about the scene struck Sara as more than just one friend comforting another. The easy way they sat spoke of intimacy. She knew they were involved but seeing it like that made it real. It felt like someone had a chokehold on her heart, squeezing the life, the hope for a happy ending right out of her.

Sara started to clear her throat, announce her presence to them, when Tristan spoke. "Fuck you, Shame."

"Now why do you want to be that way?" Shame responded. "Every word I said was the truth and you know it."

"I repeat, fuck you."

Shame chuckled, his hand flexing around the apple of Tristan's shoulder. "I would take you up on that, if I thought you actually meant it. Lord knows I need to get laid. It's a damned shame we both know who you'd rather be sticking that big cock of yours into."

There was a long pause. "How do you know what I want? Maybe I've lost my taste for pussy and prefer your tight asshole over some loose cunt."

Sara gasped. Her hand flew to her mouth to conceal the sound before it could escape and give her away. She didn't wait to find out if she'd been caught eavesdropping. She turned and fled.

Tristan and Shame both surged to their feet, turning toward the noise behind them in time to see Sara's backside disappear around the corner. "Shit," they both said in unison.

"Well, looks like you really put your foot in it this time. You better hustle after her and fix it," Shame advised.

Tristan was already moving out the door after her.

He found Sara in the basement, elbows-deep in a laundry basket. She stood with her back to him, but she held herself too straight, her posture too rigid, not to be aware of him behind her.

"I'm sorry," he blurted out. "I didn't mean it."

"Didn't mean what?" she whispered.

So that was the game she was going to play. Just pretend like she hadn't overheard anything. He'd be more than happy to let it go at that, if he didn't know his carelessly spoken words had hurt her. Hell, he may have let it go anyway, if what he'd said had been the truth.

"I didn't mean a single word you overheard, Sara. There's no way in hell that I would rather fuck Shame when I could make love to you instead."

Sara continued to search through the basket and mate socks, unwilling to face him. "Your sex life is none of my concern."

Tristan grabbed her by the shoulders and forced her around to face him. If he was going to grovel, it wasn't going to be to her ass, fine though it was. "What do you want me to say, damn it? I didn't mean it. I was pissed off, just running my mouth. I said I was sorry. What more do you want from me?"

"Nothing. You don't owe me anything, Tristan. I shouldn't have listened in on your conversation. In my defense, you were in *my* bedroom. I was just going to put away some clean clothes and happened to overhear you talking. I didn't mean to invade your privacy."

Sara paused. He could almost see the wheels turning in her mind. "I guess I owe you an apology too. If I had been aware of your new sexual preference, I wouldn't have forced you to endure sex with me."

Tristan laughed. He couldn't help himself. The idea of her forcing him to have sex with her was ludicrous.

Sara apparently didn't think it was so funny. Her jaw visibly tightened and a nerve began to tick at the corner of one eye. "I'm glad you find this so hilarious," she hissed through clenched teeth.

Tristan banked his laughter. He stalked toward her, determined to show her once and for all exactly what she did to him. He didn't stop until he was sure she couldn't wiggle her way around him. With nowhere else to go, Sara backed right up to the wall. Two short steps and the space between them was eliminated. Tristan put one hand on the wall next to her head, pinning her between him and the dryer.

He leaned in, so close he could make out the rapidly beating pulse at the base of her neck. "Give me your hand."

Sara looked at him warily. "Why?"

Tristan reached for her hand.

Sara hid them behind her back. "No."

"Yes." He grasped her hand and pressed it against the front of his pants, where his cock throbbed, long and thick for her. "Feel that? That's what you do to me. As soon as you enter the room all I can think about is working my cock inside you, fucking you until I don't know anything but the feel of you around me. Does that sound like something I'd want to do if I wasn't attracted to you, didn't want you more than my next breath of air?"

Sara's fingers curled around his shaft through the worn denim, her thumb rubbing over the sensitive head of his cock. He wanted to howl, it felt so good. Wanted to rip open his pants and feel her soft skin cupping him, kneading, building up the sweet friction that led to release. Sara pulled away and Tristan sighed in frustration. She opened her mouth and he wasn't sure if she would curse him or kiss him.

A small voice at the top of the stairs made sure he would never know. "Mom, what's for lunch? I'm hungry."

Sara's eyes narrowed. "I don't have time for whatever game you're trying to play with me, Tristan." She pushed past him and headed up the stairs. "I'll be right there, Sam."

༄༅

The hot sun beat down on Sara's back as she yanked one weed after another from her flowerbed.

Sam was busy playing with Bob, who'd miraculously shown up earlier in the day. Other than being hungry and filthy, he was fine. The dog was smarter than her. He'd sensed the creature getting ready to pounce. Had even growled and barked to warn her, but she'd been too stupid to heed the warning. And she'd paid for it. Bob had been smart and ran away.

Sam was elated to have his friend back. He pranced around the yard, throwing a stick for Bob to fetch. The dog trotted back over to him, stick in mouth, and dropped it at Sam's feet. Sam bent to retrieve it and Bob licked his hand, causing her son to giggle.

Sara smiled. Kids were extraordinary beings. While she was confused and unsure of what was happening around her, Sam was happy just to be alive and going with the flow as if nothing were out of the ordinary. It would be nice if she could follow his example.

"Mom! Mom!" Sam ran toward her, Bob panting hot on his heels. "Look, I taught Bob a trick." Sam held his hand out to the dog. "Shake," he ordered. Big brown doggy eyes stared blankly up at him. "Shake!" Sam waved his hand in front of the dog. "Come on, boy. You did it a minute ago."

"Maybe he's tired, Sam. Bob has been off having a big adventure for the last few days."

"No, Mom. He just did it. Watch."

Sam held both hands out this time and looked sternly down at his doggy pal. "Shake, Bob. I know you can do it."

Sure enough, as Sara watched, Bob jumped up on his hind legs and dropped his front paws into her child's waiting palms. Sam squealed with glee and fell to his knees, wrapping his thin arms around Bob's torso, hugging the dog to him. "See, Mom. I told you he could do it."

"Sam, let go of Bob. He's stinky. We'll have to give him a good scrubbing before you can love on him."

"Ah, Mom," Sam complained. "Bob's not stinky. He smells just like a dog's supposed to."

"You better listen to your mother, young man."

Sara startled at the sound of the gravelly voice so close behind her. She rose to her feet and turned to see Tristan standing next to an older man. He was the one who'd spoken.

The man was slightly shorter than Tristan. His salt-and-pepper hair was cut short, in what she knew men in the service called a high and tight. The square line of his jaw was covered in several days' worth of coarse gray stubble. Although he wore casual clothes, a plain white T-shirt and jeans, Sara had no problem envisioning him in full military regalia. The jeans were even ironed, a razor-sharp crease running down each pant leg.

Something about the man tugged at her memory, just out of reach, as if she'd seen him before but she couldn't quite place where.

Tristan stepped forward. "Sara, this is Commander John Ramsey. My boss." Tristan immediately began to twiddle his thumbs. What was he nervous about? That she would embarrass him in front of his boss?

Sara wiped her dirty hands off on her shorts before offering it to Tristan's boss. "Nice to meet you."

The man looked at her hand like it was a poisonous snake for an instant before grasping it between his two calloused paws. He let go of her hand almost as soon as he touched her.

"Um," Sara stammered, shooting a glance at Sam. "Why don't we go inside for a glass of ice tea? I just made a fresh batch before I gave Sam his lunch."

"Sure. That would be great," Tristan replied.

"Sam, you stay in the yard with Bob. Stay right here in the fenced area where I can see you. Okay?"

"Sure, Mom."

Sara led the men into the kitchen. Shame showed up right as she was pulling the pitcher of tea from the fridge. After pouring an extra glass for him, she sat at the table with the men, choosing to sit next to the window so she could keep an eye on Sam.

All of them looked anxious. She watched each one's mannerisms carefully. Tristan fumbled with his hands, like he didn't know what to do with them. Shame chewed on the inside of his cheek. Their boss sat unmoving, but his gaze darted around the room, never staying on one spot for long before moving on.

Sara glanced from one man to the other, none of them meeting her eyes. "Okay, one of you want to tell me what's up, or am I gonna have to try to guess?"

Tristan started to speak, but Ramsey cut him off. "You don't recognize me, do you?" he asked, facing Sara.

"No. Is there some reason I should? Have we met?"

The man winced at her question. The way his skin stretched taut over his cheekbones made him look almost pained.

"I'm sorry," Sara said, glancing around the table. "Am I missing something here? Would someone like to explain what's going on?"

"Maybe this wasn't such a good idea," Mr. Ramsey or Commander Ramsey or whatever his name was said as he got up from the table. Riffling through his pockets, he pulled out a wrinkled business card. "My number is on here. Tristan and Shame know where I'm staying if you decide to see me."

Shame followed him out. Sara assumed he was going to walk the man to the door. She waited until she heard the front door close before she rounded on Tristan. "What was all of that about?" she asked, waving the card under his nose. "Why in the world would I need to talk to your boss?"

"Calm down, Sara. Take a deep breath and really think for a minute. Doesn't the name John Ramsey sound even remotely familiar to you?"

"No."

"Think about it."

"Tristan, I don't appreciate your playing these stupid games with me. Just tell me whatever it is I'm supposed to know already."

"Fine, I'll tell you, but maybe we should go sit in the living room. It's more comfortable in there."

"No, you tell me right here. Besides, I can't watch Sam from in there."

"Okay. That man, *my boss,* is your father."

Was this supposed to be some kind of joke? "No, he isn't."

"He is, Sara. I've worked under the man for years and today is the first I've heard of this myself, so I'm just as shocked as you are, but John is your dad."

Sara shook her head. "No." Her father had walked out on her and her mother and never come back. It didn't make sense that he would come sniffing around now, when everything else in her life was going to hell in a handbasket. Even less that he could be Tristan's boss. That was just too much of a coincidence. It was almost laughable.

"Yes, he is, Sara. Quit arguing with me."

"Give me a break, Tristan. Don't you think I would recognize my own father? That man doesn't look anything like him."

"Sara, it's been over twenty years since you saw him. Don't you think he may have changed in that much time?"

"Tristan, he is not my father. This is ridiculous." Sara thought for a moment, her mind spinning on how she could call

Tristan's bluff. "I can prove it to you. I have an old photo around here somewhere of my parents. It was taken before I was born, but I'm sure you'll clearly be able to see that there's no way that man is who he claims to be."

Tristan shook his head. "Okay, Sara. Go find your picture."

Sara eyed the window. "Would you mind keeping an eye on Sam while I go look for it?"

"I'll watch him."

"All right, I'll be back in a few minutes. Make sure you don't let him get out of your sight for a single second though. You'd be surprised how much one little boy can get into while your back is turned."

"Don't worry, I'll watch him."

Sara went upstairs to the spare room where she kept all of the junk she didn't know what to do with. Several big boxes full of photos were perched on the top shelf in the closet. She dug them out and sat in the middle of the floor, boxes all around her. This was going to take some doing.

Starting with the container closest to her, Sara began to rummage through them, desperate to put an end to the speculation over her paternity. She couldn't understand why someone would claim to be her father, when they clearly weren't. It wasn't like she had anything to give anyone. No money, no nothing. It just didn't make sense.

That's how Tristan found her an hour later. She looked up and there he was, watching her with a quirky little smile on his face. "So how's the hunt going?"

"Not well. I always plan to organize these darn things but never actually seem to get around to doing it."

"How about some help? We'll find it quicker if both of us look."

"You're supposed to be outside with Sam."

"Shame's playing with him."

"Oh," Sara replied, watching Tristan fold his big body up on the floor beside her. He picked up a handful of photos, flipping through them.

A jolt of feminine awareness swept through Sara as she regarded him. He sat so close their knees were touching. She couldn't help but be aware of him. The heat radiating off his body. His scent, a potent mixture of faint cologne, soap and heady male musk. The chemistry between them sizzled, made her dizzy with longing.

Sara closed her eyes, a flash of earlier coming back to her in vivid detail. Tristan pressing her into the wall, surrounding her with over six feet of tanned muscle, his cock hard and pulsing under her hand.

Her core wept from need as her imagination played the scene out, took it farther than it had actually gone.

Tristan swept Sara off her feet, lifting her against him. Her thighs went around his waist, holding him to her. Their clothes melted away, leaving them both naked.

Tristan's thick cock slicing into her, taking her breath away with the force of his possession. Long, slow thrusts had her mewling, begging for more.

He hitched her up higher, sucking one of her nipples into the scalding, hot cavern of his mouth...

"Earth to Sara."

Sara opened her eyes, blinking at Tristan.

"Must have been some thought you were lost in, the way you were squirming around over there," he said, a knowing smile curling the corners of his mouth.

Sara blushed and would've happily disappeared into the carpet. Talk about embarrassing. Then she remembered that the best defense was a good offense. He wasn't the only one who could tease. "Wouldn't you like to know?" she asked sassily, winking at him. She couldn't stop the mischievous smile that spread across her face when Tristan's aquamarine eyes darkened, filling with heat.

Tristan didn't waste any time changing the subject when he was the uncomfortable one. "You know, I wouldn't mind seeing some of Sam's baby pictures while we're up here."

"Dig in. They're all over the place," Sara said, waving her hand at the mess around them.

"What about this one? How old was he here?"

Sara leaned in closer to get a look at the photo he held. Being so close was not a good idea. Her respiration sped up. Her nipples tightened and began to ache for attention. If either one of them moved more than an inch her mouth would be on him. She would be able to taste his skin, lose herself in his arms.

The picture he held cooled her overheated libido faster than a bath in ice water. It was a photo of her holding Sam, not long after he was born. He was swaddled in baby blankets, so covered that all you could see was the top of his bald head. Sara remembered being so worried about him not being warm enough. It was a wonder she hadn't smothered him to death with all the layers of clothes she kept on him.

Mark or maybe it was Cindy, she wasn't sure, had taken the photo in her first apartment; a cramped little loft on the bad side of town. She'd been so proud of that place. Looking back now, she saw it for what it was—a dump. Perched on a dismal secondhand couch she'd bought at the Goodwill, Sara smiled for the camera. Though she wasn't certain why, something about the photo made her cringe. It wasn't so much that she was ashamed of the way things had been for her then, she'd done the best she could, it was more the thought of Tristan seeing it.

She was proud of the woman she'd become. The girl in the picture was a train wreck. A distant part of her past better forgotten. Having Tristan see her in that light bugged her. She didn't want him to perceive her to be anything but the strong, confident woman she showed the rest of the world. Not the disaster she'd been years before.

"That was taken when Sam was about four weeks old." She sat back down across from him, wanting to put as much distance between them as she could manage.

She needed to remember that he hadn't really come home. Not in the way she'd always dreamed he would. Tristan hadn't come back for her and Sam. He was only there for his job. As soon as it was completed, he would leave. In the meantime, Sara needed to guard her heart closely or she wouldn't survive losing him for the second time.

"Would you mind if I kept this one?" he asked.

Sara had to practically sit on her hands to keep herself from ripping it away from him. Why he wanted it, she wasn't sure. It was a terrible picture. She looked like hell, as most new mothers do, and Sam was barely visible.

"I'm sure I can find you a better picture of Sam than that one. Just give me a second to dig through a few of these."

"No," Tristan said, shaking his head. "This one is fine."

Sara watched as he put the picture in his shirt pocket. She wanted to argue and take it back, give him a different one, but since she couldn't insist without appearing childish, or worse, being forced to explain herself, Sara kept her mouth shut and went back to searching for the picture she wanted.

Sara shrieked when she finally found the one she was looking for. It was fuzzy, but the picture was the only one she had of both her parents. They stood in front of an old muscle car, her father's arm around her largely pregnant mom. They looked young and happy; in love.

Another reminder that looks could be deceiving.

"Look," Sara said, waving the picture under Tristan's nose. "I told you I would find it." She held it out to him, wanting him to take it and agree that there was no way his boss could be her father.

"Sara, I don't need to see the photo to confirm what I already know. John Ramsey is your father. No decades-old snapshot is going to change the facts."

"But you said—"

"Coming up here and searching for that old picture was your idea, not mine. You need to take a good, long hard look at it. I bet it will tell you what you want to know."

Sara's shoulders drooped. "What difference does it make? Even if, and it's a *big* if, Tristan, this man is who he claims to be, why should I care? The man who fathered me was little more than a sperm donor. It's not like he stuck around to raise me. Why should I want to have anything to do with him?"

Tristan stood. "He's not asking for you to nominate him for father of the year, Sara. He only wants to help. All he's asking for in exchange is the chance to talk to you. I don't think it's so much to ask."

"He wants to help with what? Catching the vampire after me?"

"Yes," Tristan responded quickly. A little too quickly. It made her think there was something he wasn't telling her.

"Why? I still don't get why he's here now. Everything that could possibly go wrong this week has. Another absentee father showing up is the last thing I want to deal with right now."

Tristan's jaw clenched before he turned his back on her. "I'm sorry you feel that way," he spat out. "Contrary to popular belief I did not know about Sam. Whether or not you choose to believe that, is up to you. Maybe if I'd been told about my son, things would have been different. I can't change the past, so I guess we'll never know. Nevertheless, if I hear you imply one more time that I abandoned my son I'm going to take you over my knee and tan your ass."

"Excuse me? You think you're going to do what?" Sara said, rising to her feet, equal parts anger and hurt thrumming through her blood. "You are not my keeper, Tristan McKade! I determine my actions, not you. If you don't like that then you crawl back under whatever rock you've been hiding under for the last six years."

By the time Sara was finished she was right up in his face, her index finger poking his chest. She had no memory of crossing the room after him. Angry tears filled her eyes as she looked up at Tristan. A dumbfounded expression was on his face, like he wasn't sure whether he wanted to kiss her or strangle her.

Sara didn't wait to see which he chose. She shoved past him, hurrying out of the room. The maelstrom of emotions she felt scared her. They were so strong, like a ticking bomb ready to blow at the slightest additional provocation. All she knew was that she needed to get away from Tristan before she did something she would regret later. Like kill him, or sleep with him again. Either way she'd be screwed.

Sara grabbed her purse as she went out the front door. She ignored Shame's curious gaze as she herded Sam into the rear of the car and backed out of the driveway.

Chapter Twelve

Tristan let the curtain fall back over the window. Sara sure hadn't wasted any time trying to get away from him. He wasn't even sure what he'd done to piss her off. One minute he was the one doing the lecturing and the next—*bam*—she was all over his ass.

He understood why she was upset, but while he hadn't expected a mushy talk-show reunion, neither had he foreseen her adamant refusal to believe Ramsey was really her father.

Earlier that morning, Tristan had returned to his and Shame's apartment and discovered an email awaiting them from Commander Ramsey. The brusque tone of the email, baldly stating a time and location for them to meet, sent Tristan into a tailspin of worry. He'd been terrified that Ramsey had learned about his interaction with Sara. Imagine his surprise, when he and Shame had met with their boss and found out that not only did he know about it, he approved. The long discussion that followed, including Ramsey's confession about being Sara's father, was surreal to say the least.

When the man asked them to intervene on his behalf, it had seemed like a piece of cake. Of course he and Shame had given Ramsey a chance to explain himself before they questioned his motives. Sara hadn't done that. Not that he and Shame didn't have their own reasons for getting involved. They had something to gain by cooperating. In a roundabout way, Sara did too, she just didn't realize it yet. While he and Shame had a once-in-a-lifetime chance to regain their lives, Sara would receive something else. *Him.*

Their boss offered to help them reclaim their freedom in exchange for their cooperation. With him on their side they could get out, regain their normal lives again. The fact that Tristan getting his life back meant that he would be able to stick around, take care of Sara and Sam, only seemed to sweeten the deal for Ramsey.

With the way things were going now though, Tristan wasn't sure if Sara would want him sticking around. The way she was acting toward him made Tristan think she would be more than happy to kick his ass to the curb, sooner rather than later.

ಬಿಂ

After spending most of the day at the park, letting Sam run circles around her on the playground, they ended up in the last place she expected. Sitting in the car, outside of the hotel John Ramsey was staying in.

While Sam sawed logs in the back, Sara tried to work up the courage to go into the hotel. A knock sounded on the driver's side window and Sara's head shot up and swiveled around. On the opposite side of the window, Shame's amused green gaze met her wide-eyed stare. She'd been so engrossed in her thoughts that she hadn't heard him approach the car. Sara rolled down the window. "Want to let me know how you found me? And keep your voice down, I don't want to wake Sam."

Shame's gaze wandered into the backseat, where Sam lay snoring, before returning to her. He leaned down, his hands braced on the window's edge. "Easy. There's a GPS on your car."

"There's a what on my car?"

"A tracking device. Tristan had me put it on right after you were attacked."

"Nice of you to tell me," she said smartly.

"Tristan and I are supposed to be protecting you. In case you've forgotten, there's one dangerous damn vampire out there somewhere looking for your ass. We couldn't very well just let you run willy-nilly all over the place, now could we?"

Jesus, with everything else going on she'd somehow managed to forget about that. How could she forget someone…something was trying to kill her? It didn't seem possible, but she had.

"You gonna go up?" he asked, nodding at the hotel.

"I can't. I don't know his room number."

"Mm-hmm," Shame murmured. "And if I tell you his room number? What excuse are you going to come up with then?"

"I don't know," she reluctantly admitted.

"I never would have pegged you for a coward, Sara. I could have sworn you had more pluck than that."

"Kiss my ass, Shame." If his intention had been to get her ire back up then he was doing a bang-up job of it.

"Mighty tempting, but I'd hate to piss off Tristan. I don't think he'd appreciate any slap and tickle going on without him."

"Poor Shame, you can't do anything without Tristan's permission, can you? Isn't it possible for you to ever do *anything* without asking first? I bet you have to wait to wipe your ass until he tells you it's okay."

Shame bent over double, laughing. It wasn't the reaction she had been expecting. When the guffaws slowed he stood back up, shaking his head at her. "You're hilarious."

Sara was at a loss. What did she have to do to get him to leave her alone?

"You can try to change the subject all you like, but we both know why you're out here sitting in your car."

"Why?"

"Because you're chicken."

"I am not chicken."

"*Bwack, bwack, bwack.*" Shame flapped his arms as he squawked.

"Whatever, Shame. Like I really care what you think."

"Just go up and talk to the man. His bark is worse than his bite. I promise."

"You make him sound so pleasant to be around," Sara said sarcastically.

"Well, he's not, but that doesn't mean you shouldn't hear him out. There are things he can tell you that Tristan and I haven't been able to."

That got her attention. "Like what?"

"Anything you want to know I imagine."

"Why would he be willing to tell me what the two of you can't?"

"Apparently the agency is putting him out to pasture. After all his years of service they're making him retire. They want someone younger to take his place."

"So he's pissed off at being forced into retirement and wants to spill his beans to me?"

"Yep, that about sums it up. The rest he can tell you himself, if you let him."

That made her mind up for her. She didn't necessarily want to talk to him about his paternity issues. She didn't care about that. But she wasn't about to pass up the chance to quiz him about Tristan. Finding out the stuff Tristan had withheld from her was too tempting an offer to turn down.

Innate curiosity was one of her biggest personality flaws. If curiosity killed the cat then Sara figured she would have been sliced, diced and pureed by this point in her life.

Sam was asleep in the back of the car. Shame offered to keep an eye on Sam while she went in, but Sara refused. It wasn't that she didn't trust Shame, she just felt better keeping her son with her. When she insisted on taking him in, Shame offered to carry her heavy son so she wouldn't have to wake him. To that, she readily agreed. At not quite sixty pounds he was too much for her to carry anymore.

Ramsey didn't seem surprised to see her when he opened the door a moment later, making Sara think he had been given advance notice of her arrival, which bugged her. Why should he have any warning of her arrival when she hadn't had any for his? It annoyed her that the man could look so calm and put together while she had a virtual war zone raging between her ears.

Shame carried Sam into the suite's bedroom to finish out his nap, while Sara silently followed Ramsey over to a sitting area which consisted of a single green plaid couch and chair. He sat on one corner of the long couch, leaving plenty of room for her to sit beside him. Sara sat in the chair across from him instead.

Ramsey stared at her for an untold number of minutes. Since she wasn't wearing a watch, she didn't know how long it went on, but it felt like forever. Her patience began to wear thin. "You wanted to talk to me. So here I am. Talk." Sara knew she was being rude, but couldn't help it. If this man was her father, then that made him the asshole who'd abandoned she and her mother. The man her mother had pined away for until she couldn't stand the loneliness and had taken her own life.

Sara didn't owe him a damn thing.

He cleared his throat, shooting her a beseeching glance. "I'm not asking you to forgive or even forget the things that have happened in the past. I know it wasn't easy for you after Audrey died. Part of that was my fault, by not being there. All I ask is that you hear me out. I'd like to tell you my side of things before you form any opinions about me."

"You think I haven't already formed an opinion about you? Like I haven't had any time in the last two decades to think about it?"

"I just meant that I would like the chance to explain before you form any new ones."

"Fine," Sara replied shortly. "How do I even know you are who you claim to be?"

"My name is on your birth certificate."

"I'm sure there is more than one man named John Ramsey in this country."

"All right. Your birthday is August first. Your mother's name was Audrey Rose. We named you after my mother Sarah and since we couldn't think of a good middle name I talked your mother into using hers. That's how you came to be Sara Rose."

"Most of that can be found in public record, you could have made the rest up."

"You were born with a small heart-shaped birthmark on your behind. Another strawberry-shaped one on the inside of your right thigh."

"Tristan could have told you that." Sara was getting a perverse satisfaction out of making him uncomfortable.

"He didn't," Ramsey said, tugging on his collar.

"There's no way I can know that for sure."

"Fine." He was silent for a moment. "Right before I left, I gave your mother a locket. Instead of putting photos in it like most people, she kept a lock of our entwined hair inside it."

Sara rubbed her chest, where the locket lay safe between her breasts. He couldn't know that unless he'd been the one to do it. The hair clippings were long gone, buried with her mom, but Sara had kept the locket. It was always with her, she never took it off. Tristan knew about the locket itself, but not the locks of hair once inside.

The man really was her father. Why did that make her want to strike out at him more?

"Does that convince you?"

Sara nodded. A million questions she'd always wanted answered filtered through her mind. She didn't ask any of them. Her childhood musings could continue to go unanswered. She could only think of one question that was relevant at the moment.

"Why?" she asked. "Why are you contacting me now, after all these years?"

"There never seemed to be a good time before."

"And you're saying that you think now, with everything that's already going on, is a good time for you to drop this bomb in my lap?"

"This opportunity is the best one I've found. Once I have explained you will understand better."

Sara sat back against the chair, her arms crossed over her chest. "I'm all ears."

"As you already know, Shame and Tristan work under my direction. What you don't know is how or why that came to pass." He took a deep breath, his eyes glazing over in a faraway look.

"When I met your mother I was involved in a classified research program. By that time I'd been involved in the project for the better part of a decade. What started out as recumbent DNA research with my mentor, Steven Hawkins, had morphed into full-scale human cloning. Way ahead of our time, we were already working on human cloning specifically for use in organ transplantation. In the seventies most other scientists were just beginning to work on genetic manipulation. Together, Steven and I far surpassed that."

Sara opened her mouth, ready to say bullshit, but stopped when he held a hand up, effectively shushing her.

"As I was saying, we were already ahead of the game when I met your mom. I told her what I told everyone else, that I was a research assistant helping to develop new prescription drugs. She took me at my word and let it go. There was no reason for her to suspect anything else."

"Why lie about it?" Sara asked.

"I'm sure you remember the controversy surrounding Dolly, the first successfully cloned sheep in '96. Imagine what it would have been like for the public to know scientists were already working on humans over twenty years earlier. The religious outrage over the world's first healthy delivery of an IVF baby in '77 was enough to warn us off going public."

"Okay, I get it. Go on," Sara said. She was impatient to hear what all this had to do with her mother and Tristan.

"So we kept our work quiet. For several years I was able to maintain a normal life with Audrey, no one being the wiser about my secret career choice. When you were about two, Steven suffered a massive stroke and passed away. Being the only other person working on our project it was only natural that I would take it over.

"After all my hard work it was a great opportunity. One I couldn't let go, even when I was informed by the men in charge that the labs were going to be transferred to a more secure location in a different state. Because of security issues all scientists working on the project were expected to live within the compound."

"And that's when you left," Sara stated flatly.

"Yes. I chose to continue my life's work rather than stay behind with your mother and you. It was the only choice for me. It was my chance to make a difference, be someone. Nothing was more important than the project."

He smiled and Sara wanted to smack it right off his face. Didn't he even realize what he'd said? She didn't want to let it bother her, but it did. He made it sound like their well-being was about as inconsequential as dirt under his fingernail.

"Is there a point you're getting at? I mean besides how unimportant my mother and I were to you."

His face grew ruddy at her snarky rephrasing of his words. Sara wanted to believe he was ashamed of himself, but it was doubtful.

"I'm getting there if you'll let me continue. I'd like to get it all out while I have the chance."

Sara pressed her lips together and waved him on. She would listen to what he had to say. As soon as he finished she would take her son and leave, knowing she'd met her father and dismissed him as someone she didn't want in her life.

"In the late nineties we lost our funding. In a mad scramble to keep our project alive I made the mistake of accepting a proposal from the military. At the time it seemed like a good idea. Knowing what I know now..." He waved the thought away before continuing.

"Anyway the government insisted that we limit our test subjects to the men and women in the military who would volunteer to be our guinea pigs. The problem was we didn't receive any volunteers. The good men and women of the armed forces weren't willing to devote their bodies to science.

"Without them, our work was at a standstill. We were ready to apply our knowledge to live subjects, but we didn't have any. The higher-ups were breathing down our necks to produce results. The number of supernatural crimes tripled, causing them to be in dire need of the bioengineered soldiers we promised them.

"At that time, we made a unanimous decision. Since we had no live volunteers to work with, we needed to recruit men in some other way. It was decided that we would screen wounded soldiers for the background we needed. The only staunch requirement was that the men selected be single, with no known family members to come looking for them if something went wrong."

Sara's mind raced ahead of his words. "No," she shouted. It was obvious where he was heading. God help her, she didn't want to hear it. Not from this unfeeling monster. She scooted to the edge of her chair and shook her head. "I've heard enough. Stop."

Ramsey ignored her and continued. "When they brought in the first group of soldiers, Tristan and Shame were among the mortally wounded. I ran the required background checks on them both and found out who Tristan was to you. I broke my own rules to keep him and his friend alive, even knowing it would someday come back to bite me in the ass. I know it's no excuse, but Tristan would truly be dead if not for the program's intervention. It doesn't make up for the years you've lost, but—"

Sara jumped up out of the chair and loomed over him. "Shut up. Just shut the hell up. How can you sit there and tell me you did this for me? What kind of sick joke is this? You took him from me, from his son, and forced him to fake his own death so you could make a quick buck from the government. What kind of monster are you?"

Ramsey reached for her hand, missing it as she jerked out of his reach. "You have to try to understand, Sara."

"Fuck that. I don't have to understand anything. And I don't have to stand here and listen to any more of your bullshit." Sara stormed out of the room to collect her son. As soon as she had Sam, she was getting the hell out of there.

Chapter Thirteen

Sara sat on the couch, pouting. She'd hurried home, breaking every speed limit, only to find the house silent and empty, Tristan nowhere to be found.

She'd spent the evening with her son, trying to keep her pessimistic mind from traveling down paths better left alone. When the time came to put Sam to bed, Sara was grateful for it. Only then did she allow herself to contemplate her fears.

Neither man, Shame nor Tristan, had shown up that evening. She knew Ramsey—she refused to use the word Father—was their boss. If her behavior with him that evening caused them to be pulled from the case and reassigned elsewhere, she'd never be able to forgive herself. Learning that Tristan hadn't had a choice in leaving her, only to have him ripped away from her again before she even had the chance to tell him she still loved him, qualified as cruel and unusual torture.

She prayed her fears were unfounded. That Tristan was only out, doing whatever it was he did when he left the house and that he'd come home soon, before what little hope she clung to was lost.

The screen door squeaked, banged back against the siding, and Sara jumped from the couch, her eyes wide, her heart filling with promise. She stood still as a statue, waiting for the front door to open and his tall form to fill the arch.

The screen slammed back into the door with a loud rattle.

Only the wind. Damn.

Sara exhaled and bit into her bottom lip. Who was she kidding? He wasn't coming back. She wasn't going to get that lucky. Forcing herself across the room, Sara yanked open the door, intent on re-latching the screen so it wouldn't fly open again.

Tristan and Shame stood on the porch. Her heart lurched, stopping for a split second before roaring back to life and beating harder, with renewed purpose.

Sara squealed and launched herself at Tristan, throwing her arms around his waist. He stumbled back a step before regaining his balance. Sara didn't care. They could have fallen face first into the hedge and it wouldn't have mattered.

"Whoa," he said. "What's all this about?"

Tears welled behind her eyes and she buried her face in Tristan's chest to hide them. She rubbed her face against the soft cotton of the shirt he wore, wiping away the wetness, before meeting his questioning gaze.

The warmth she saw there, in his eyes, called out to her and filled her with an answering heat that couldn't be denied. One she didn't want to deny. Sara leaned against him for support and rose up on tiptoe to press her lips against his. Sara kissed him hungrily, desperate to convey all her feelings through the join of their lips. Tristan kissed her back, but his body remained stiff and uncommunicative.

Sara pulled her mouth from his and saw only confusion written on his face. Her mouth opened and an outpour tumbled forth. "I was so worried about you. Terrified you wouldn't come home." Her voice caught on the last word, betraying her brittle emotions. "When I got back and you weren't here and then Shame never came back, I thought the two of you had moved on." Sara spared a glance for Shame standing off to the side by himself. "That you'd left me."

A calloused thumb traced the contours of Sara's jaw. It whispered over her skin, leaving goose bumps in its wake. He tilted her chin up, his lips swooping down to taste hers. Sara closed her eyes and gave herself over to the kiss. His tongue slipped between her lips, plunging past her teeth to parry with her own.

An involuntary moan escaped her mouth when one hard hand gripped her behind, squeezing. Sara shifted closer, wiggling against him. She wanted to crawl inside his skin and make her home there. Be one with this man, her man, for all eternity. She wanted to jump him and climb him like a tree. Impale herself on the thick cock swelling ever larger against her stomach in evidence of his desire for her. The ache between her thighs increased, throbbing and clenching emptily.

Tristan ended the kiss and Sara whimpered. He halted, their mouths separated by the merest of centimeters. Hot air caressed her moist lips as he spoke. "I'm not going anywhere, Sara."

She stepped away, immediately missing the warmth of his big body pressed against hers. What did he mean? He wasn't going anywhere for now or forever? She swallowed the questions down before they could escape her mouth. She didn't want to hear his answer. Was too afraid of what it would be.

As the world around them came back into focus, heat suffused Sara's face. They were outside, highlighted by the bright porch light they stood beneath. She cast a bashful look

Shame's way, only then remembering that he was present. Shame looked right back at her, a smile on his face. Sara's lips curved up at the corners in reply. Or they started to before she noticed that his usually friendly smile stopped short of his eyes. The emotion she read there was not the happiness for them that she'd thought to find. It was closer to envy.

Sara's heart went out to him. She felt guilty for being so short-sighted. While she'd spent most of the evening thinking about Tristan's predicament, she hadn't once thought of Shame. He was in the same situation, wasn't he? Shame was a good man. He deserved to have someone love him every bit as much as she loved Tristan.

"Maybe we should take our little sideshow into the house. I'm sure you don't want your neighbors to get the wrong idea about things," Tristan said.

"You're right. I think they've gotten enough of a show this evening," Sara agreed.

She went inside ahead of the men, feeling their inquisitive eyes on her back. Sara bypassed the furniture, choosing to stand at the base of the stairs instead.

"Um...Tristan, could we talk?" Sara tugged self-consciously at the pajama top she wore. She wished she'd worn something more alluring, anything but the faded short set she had on. Nobody in their right mind would consider yellow cotton pajamas covered in pink stars sexy.

"Sure," he replied, plopping down on the couch next to Shame.

Sara looked pointedly at Tristan, nodded in Shame's direction and then at the stairs. He returned a blank stare. So much for being subtle. She didn't want to come out and say she needed to be alone with him, as in get rid of Shame, but he wasn't getting her signals. "We could go upstairs," she suggested.

"I think she's trying to get you alone, bud," Shame helpfully pointed out.

His cheeks tinged with pink, Tristan muttered a quick "Thanks" to Shame as he rose to his feet.

ಬಿಂ

Tristan didn't know what was going on. The only thing he was positive of was that Sara confused the hell out of him.

Earlier, she'd been ready to kill him, and now she seemed to lean more toward fucking him than anything else. Not that he was complaining. Hell no. He just wanted to be clear about it before he said or did anything else to piss her off.

"So," he said, pacing back and forth in front of Sara, who sat casually leaning back on her bed. "What do you want to talk to me about?"

"I talked to your boss this evening."

"Yeah?" *And?*

"He told me some pretty interesting things. I guess I just wanted you to confirm or deny what he said. I'm not sure how much of what he said was the truth."

Sara tugged at her top for the umpteenth time, pulling it down low enough he could see the upper swell of her breasts and make out the shadowed valley between them. Tristan swallowed the lump forming in his throat at the sight. What he wouldn't give to bury his face between her breasts, lave at the rosy nipples crowning them. He felt his cock stir at the image and mentally cursed his vivid imagination.

"What do you want to know?" he asked.

"Why didn't you come home to me?"

"I already answered that question, Sara. I wasn't given a choice."

"Yes, you did. But you didn't tell me what happened. You said you couldn't tell me that part. Remember?"

Tristan nodded. Where was she going with this?

"Now you can." Sara eased backward a little more, baring a line of silky skin between her top and her shorts. He had an insane urge to bend over her and lick it.

"What do you want to hear, Sara? I wanted to come back to you. I would have, if I'd had any choice at the time. I didn't. I don't know what else you want me to say."

When she didn't say anything, Tristan began to get nervous. What was the little minx up to? He turned and pretended to look out the window while he adjusted the bulge in his pants. She didn't need any more evidence of how strongly she affected him.

"Is that all you wanted?" Tristan asked, his back to Sara.

"No," she said, her voice low.

"What else then?" He turned to face her, not sure how much more interrogation he could stand. Pictures of their making love in the very bed she lounged on assaulted him, one after another. Him licking her sweet pussy. Her hot little tongue lapping at his balls. Sara moaning and bucking beneath him as he fed his cock into her tight sheath. All the blood in his body raced straight to his dick, engorging it to the point of pain.

Sara toyed nervously with a lock of her hair. "Just a few questions, is all. There are a few things I've been curious about."

He watched Sara suck her bottom lip into her mouth and chew on it, then release it all wet and shiny. She was trying to kill him. He was literally going to die if he didn't get some relief soon. His cock had been at attention all day, even while she was gone, and seeing her half-naked, saucily laying back on the mattress caused his mouth to water and his balls to ache.

Tristan didn't want to ask but he couldn't help himself. "What do you want to know?" As soon as he asked he wanted to kick himself in the ass. She'd made it clear earlier that she didn't want to have anything to do with him. Frankly, after everything that happened, he couldn't really blame her. Which didn't explain why he was still in her room when he should have been hightailing it to the bathroom for a much-needed cold shower.

Sara fidgeted before speaking. "I um...couldn't help but notice that you and Shame are pretty tight. I guess what I want to know is exactly how *tight* the two of you are?"

Shit. How was he supposed to put his friendship with Shame into words? What exactly would he say—that they were lovers, fuck-buddies? Neither of those descriptions quite fit.

"I guess I would say that Shame and I are friends with privileges."

"Friends with privileges, huh? Are you...um, serious?"

What did she mean by that? "Huh?"

"Would you say you're better *friends* than say...you and me?"

Tristan paced in front of the window. What was she asking? "You and I aren't friends."

Sara recoiled as if he'd slapped her.

She looked so sweet, so wary, as she stared at up at him, her eyes full of questions. He moved to the edge of the bed, towering over her. "Sara, I would say we're a lot more than friends. Wouldn't you?"

His fingers itched to touch her, to close the space between them. He didn't resist his impulses. Tristan's knuckles brushed away a wily, auburn curl sticking to her face, his hand lingering over the soft skin of her cheek.

Emotions long bottled broke open, gushing unrestrained to the surface. Holding them back was impossible. "I love you, Sara. I want to be a lot more than just your friend. I want to be your lover, your confidant, the person you lean on when things get rough. If you'll have me, I want to be your husband."

When he finished speaking Sara's eyes glittered with unshed moisture. One fat teardrop slid from her eye and streaked down her face. He wiped it away with the pad of his thumb. "Enough of that. I think you've shed enough tears. No more crying."

Sara caught him around the waist and tackled him to the bed. Tristan found himself flat on his back, staring up into Sara's beautiful, expressive face. He could easily read all the emotions she felt. Love. Desire. Need.

Sara climbed astride him, her legs on either side of his hips. Her heat soaked through his clothes, setting him afire. Leaning over, she sought his mouth out with her own. Their lips touched, a match to the explosive flame of his passion. Tongues collided, rubbing and gliding over one another, and they both groaned in unison. Tristan tasted the salt of her tears, her rising ardor and swore he could even feel her soul by the very depth of her kiss. It was too much at once, more than he could take.

Tearing his mouth from hers, he ran his lips over the arch of her throat, the silky skin of her shoulder. "God, Sara. I need you so bad," he breathed into her ear as he nipped the lobe, flicked it with his tongue.

Their pelvises smashed together, grinding. Tristan's hips arched up against the delicious friction, pressing harder. He wanted...needed...

Sara seemed to know. She moved down his body, every inch of her rubbing over him, teasing him. Finding the snap on his jeans, she worked it open and snaked her hand inside, stroking his cock and fondling his balls.

Cool air washed over his hot flesh as she freed him of his trousers. Sara scrambled off his lap and moved to the foot of the bed, taking his jeans and boxers with her. There she froze, looking him over from head to toe.

Her gaze landed on his cock and it jumped, preening for her attention. Tristan squirmed under her intense appraisal, slick beads of pre-come weeping from his cock in anticipation of her touch.

Naked from the waist down, he awaited her next move. It was her turn to have the upper hand and he gladly relinquished control to her. Gloried in the fact that she wanted it.

She crawled between his legs, her breasts brushing his thighs. Her pink tongue darted out, flicking over the hair-roughened inside of his thighs and Tristan thought his head was going to blow.

She reached the apex between his legs, her finger tracing a lazy figure eight over his balls. "You stopped me the last time," she whispered absently, watching her fingers skim over him. "I want to make love to you. Show you how much I still love you."

Tristan's breath caught in his throat. It was a damn cliché, but those four little words, I still love you, had the power to bring him to his knees. Until they passed her lips he hadn't known how much he needed to hear her say them. How much her love meant to him.

Sara loved him. He wanted to shout it to the world.

All thoughts of the rest of the world vanished when her thumb swirled over the tip of him, spreading the bead of moisture she found there. The fat head of his cock pulsed, yearning for relief.

"Mmm...Sara." Her name came out as a plea. The tight grip of her fist engulfed him. She pumped up and down his shaft, her palm slick with the natural lubrication his body provided. Sparks flashed behind Tristan's closed eyes.

Sara shifted. Her breath brushed over the hypersensitive tip of his dick as she spoke. "I want to taste you. Love you with my mouth. Let me?"

"Oh, yeah. Suck me, Sara. Wrap those sexy lips around my cock and suck me. I want you to. So much."

Her hot mouth surrounded his cock, engulfing him straight down to the root. Tristan cried out, his hips arching into her. Up and down, over and over, she took him in. Slurping noises filled the room as she enthusiastically worked him over, sucking, licking, driving him insane. Her tongue swiped over the crown, lingering to lave at the grooved depression under it.

Tristan gritted his teeth, trying to hold back the orgasm gaining momentum in his balls. He wasn't going to last much longer if he didn't stop her soon. "My balls..." he pleaded. "Lick my balls."

Sara moaned against his cock, her throat vibrating around him. His cock slid free of her mouth, glistening wetly from her saliva. The sight alone was enough to send him into a downward spiral. He wanted to come so bad.

Propping himself up on his elbows, Tristan avidly watched her scoot down to lay between his spread legs. Her tongue skimmed her bee-stung lips. Tristan writhed against the sheets, already able to feel her mouth upon him. Then it was there, her tongue fluttering over his tightly drawn sac, licking and nudging his desire impossibly higher.

Sara's eyes twinkled mischievously. One of her hands snaked down between her legs and slid through the wet folds of her pussy. Tristan cursed, his eyes flying skyward to look at the ceiling. Sara touching herself was more than he could take. If he watched her pleasure herself there would be no stopping the climax already beating at the base of his cock, demanding release.

He felt her wet finger against him an instant too late to voice his opposition. It pressed against his anus and wiggled its way past the resistant ring of muscle, sliding in deep to caress the walnut-shaped protrusion of his prostate. His breath coming in rough gasps, Tristan rose up off the bed. He grabbed Sara under the arms and dragged her up his body. "I can't wait... Ride me."

Sara's eyes widened at the terse command, but she complied, her hips lifting over him. Grasping his cock, she aimed him toward heaven and delivered, swallowing his full length in one hard downward thrust.

Tristan couldn't contain the ragged cry of ecstasy that spilled from his mouth as she immersed him in tight, wet heat. Sara groaned as well, the husky timbre of her moan setting him on edge.

Sara slammed up and down on his shaft, impaling herself on him over and over. Her breasts bounced with each forceful lunge. "Oh God! Tristan, you feel so good."

Wanting to make her feel better than good, he reached between their bodies and slid his fingers between the swollen lips of her sex, searching for the small bundle of nerves hidden at the top. Her clit was hard, protruding out of its protective covering. Tristan circled it lightly, repeatedly, with the calloused edge of his thumb.

The walls of her pussy clenched around him, telling him she was close. So was he. He could feel the come churning inside him, rising up. He wanted her to let go first, to feel her orgasm burst over her, while she rode him. Make her scream in bliss before he took his ease.

Sara's pelvis rose up, slammed down. Her hips rotated against him and he lost the battle. In a desperate attempt to make her come first he rubbed harder, faster, tightening the circles over her clit, pressing down on it.

"Oh, damn! Don't stop, Tristan…I'm gonna…" The first contraction of her climax hit, her honeyed walls squeezing down on his cock.

Tristan shouted her name as he filled her with his seed.

Sara collapsed into a boneless heap on Tristan's chest. Damn, the man really knew how to rock her world. She spent a moment wallowing in the afterglow, basking in the love words they exchanged, until the kernel of curiosity brewing about Tristan and Shame's relationship got the better of her.

"Tristan?"

Tristan kissed the top of her head. "Hmm?"

"What's it like?"

"What?"

"Making love to another man."

Tristan laughed. "I wouldn't exactly call it love-making. That's what we share. With Shame it was more like sport fucking, just doing it to get off, to feel something besides my hand."

Sara rubbed her cheek over Tristan's chest, enjoying the coarse feel of his hair against her skin. "That's not what I meant. I mean, what does it *feel* like?"

She felt Tristan swallow. He was silent for a moment, and then finally answered. "What do you want to know?"

"Did you do him, let him fuck you, or both? I'm just curious about what it felt like, is all. I've always wondered what the attraction to anal sex was all about. I've never done it, you know." Her cheeks heated. "Anal."

Tristan's arms tightened around her, his hand rubbing small circles over her side. "Does that mean you want to?"

Sara shrugged. "Maybe. You didn't answer my question."

"Damn, you caught me."

Sara laughed and poked him in the stomach. "Well, answer the question."

"We did both."

"And? What did it feel like?"

"I don't know. It hurts a little, at first, burns. Then it eases up and feels good. It's hard to describe. I was usually the one doing Shame because he usually had a woman beneath him."

"A woman? Why didn't you just share her?"

"We could have. I just didn't want to. You're the only woman I wanted. If I couldn't have you…no one else appealed to me."

An indescribable joy filled Sara at his words. She twisted her neck and leaned up to kiss Tristan. "I love you." It was hard to fathom a man giving up sex with women, but she believed him. He had no reason to lie about it. After all, who was she to judge? She'd been two steps away from marrying another man when he'd come storming back into her life.

Tristan wiped her hair out of her face and pressed his lips to hers, kissing her slow and sweet. "I love you too, princess."

Sara squirmed, Tristan's come uncomfortably slicking her thighs. "I need to clean up. You made a mess all over me."

Tristan laughed. "You asked for it."

She kissed him one last time before scrambling off the bed. "So I did. I'll be right back."

Chapter Fourteen

Sara stared at herself in the mirror, rehearsing what she'd say to Tristan once she left the safety of the bathroom. It wasn't everyday a woman proposed having a three-way with her lover and his best friend. Nor was it a common practice in her neck of the woods to admit to being turned-on by the prospect of observing the man she loved take it up the ass. Nevertheless, it did turn her on. To the point where she found herself flushed and had to clench her thighs in an effort to ease the persistent throb between her legs.

Hearing Tristan talk about fucking Shame tripped her trigger in a big way. Even more titillating was the thought of being in the center of all that testosterone, having both men's attention focused on pleasing her alone. Fucking them both would be the realization of every one of her taboo fantasies all wrapped into one blazingly hot night. The fact that what she wanted was so naughty only upped her desire to follow through with it.

Sara turned on the faucet and splashed a handful of icy water over her flushed cheeks. She grabbed her toothbrush off the mantle and applied toothpaste, scrubbing away at her teeth to buy a few more minutes respite until she went for it. The worst Tristan could do was say no and she wouldn't know how he reacted until she asked. She just needed a minute more to compose herself, and then she was going to do it.

☼☼

Jesus. When Sara said she needed to clean up, she wasn't kidding. She'd been in the damn bathroom forever. Okay, so maybe it'd only been twenty minutes, but it *felt* like forever. If she took much longer he was going to go in and drag her out. Tristan's cock was hard as a spike and he knew just where he wanted to put it. Visions of Sara's sexy heart-shaped ass filled his mind. He could hardly wait to part the fleshy globes of her backside, see her rosebud pull open, allowing him to sink inch by slow inch inside until the full length of his cock was encased in the tight vise of her ass.

Damn it! He wished she would hurry up. It couldn't take that long to wash up. Hell, there wasn't that much of her to wash.

Tristan sat up on the edge of the bed, shooting a glance at the door. Fuck it. He couldn't wait any longer.

Tristan stood, in the process of pulling on his jeans, when Sara walked into the room. She smiled brightly, but something about her expression looked a little…off. Before he could give it much thought she sauntered over and wrapped her arms around him, hugging him tightly.

Tristan kissed her forehead, buried his nose in her hair. The shampoo she used smelled of peaches and made him think of summer. "I was starting to think you had gotten lost in there."

"Sorry, I was just taking my time."

"Well I'm glad you finally came out. I was ready to come in after you. I missed you. T junior missed you too."

Sara glanced down at the front of his pants. His cock rose firm and heavy through the opening. "I can see that." She grabbed his dick and gave it a playful tug. "You know I wasn't gone that long. From the look of this monster you would think it had been days."

Tristan groaned at the feel of her soft fingers around him. "Felt like days, baby. I have a lot of time to make up for."

"I know you do, honey. In fact, I know just how you can make up for lost time."

Tristan eyed her suspiciously. "What do you have in mind?"

She inhaled deeply, let the breath out slowly. "I want to watch you and Shame have sex."

Tristan felt his mouth flap open at her request. It was the last thing he'd expected her to say. His mind ran a hundred miles an hour picturing all the kinky things the three of them could do together. Would it turn her on to see him fuck Shame? See Shame fuck him?

Then he remembered the woman he was thinking about. Sara. "Hell no."

"Why not? It's not like the two of you haven't done it with other women and, well, it turns me on just thinking about it. There's something so sexy about two beautiful men, together. And I was hoping that afterward, maybe, I could join in." Sara's hand stroked his stiff rod harder, faster. "Just picture it, the three of us, together, touching and kissing, making love. It would be so good. I've always fantasized about being with two big, strong, sexy men at the same time. You could make it a reality if you wanted to."

Sara leaned up and kissed him. Her tongue massaged the seam of his lips and parted them, darting inside to glide over his. With a groan, Tristan sank into her kiss, the intoxicating taste of her bursting through his senses. He wrapped his arms around her and pulled her flush against him.

Tristan felt himself caving in and it didn't matter. He'd forgotten why he was so opposed to the idea in the first place.

Chapter Fifteen

Sara sat on the end of the bed, anxiously waiting, while Tristan went in search of Shame. Her nerves were stretched taut, anticipation warring with caution. Her subconscious waffled back and forth, wondering if she'd made a mistake. The opportunity to experience something so naughty, something she never imagined would happen to her in her wildest fantasies, was surreal. Part of her gloried in the ability to share her desires with the man she loved, while a contrary bit of her wondered if she wasn't taking things too far, asking too much from Tristan too soon. They'd only just found each other again after so long and she didn't want to do anything to screw it up. Such a stigma was placed on women with strong desires. If she went through with this, and made love to both men, would Tristan somehow think less of her?

She was just about to change her mind and chicken out when Tristan waltzed into the room with Shame at his side. Sara met Tristan's eyes, saw the unspoken hunger in his gaze, the excited flush to his sharp cheekbones, and felt her doubt fade away.

She took in their rugged demeanor, their equally strong bodies, and fresh doubts assaulted her. Maybe this hadn't been such a good idea after all. Some fantasies might be meant to stay just that, fantasies. From the way they were built, to the lust apparent on both their ruggedly handsome faces, there was a good chance she wouldn't be able to handle them. Separate, it was a no-brainer, but together? She had a feeling they would be too much for her. Both men were bare-chested. Their jeans rode low on their hips, exposing the smooth jut of hipbones over denim. Shame was molded very similar to Tristan, but with slight differences. He was a little taller, a touch more broad across his shoulders. While Sara could spend days with her fingers buried in the silky hair covering Tristan's chest, seeing Shame's bare one affected her almost as much. She wanted to lick it, run her tongue over his firm pecs, down into the hollow between his ridged ab muscles. If the bulge beneath the tight denim was any indication, Sara was going to be in trouble. Shame looked to be every bit as big as Tristan, maybe more so.

Drool pooled in the corners of her mouth. When she looked back up Shame winked at her, a sensuous smile twisting up the corners of his lips. Sara's face flamed. She stiffened her back, tightening her resolve. If she was going to go through with this she would have to let go of her embarrassment. She winked back.

Shame slapped Tristan on the back, laughing. "Looks like you're going to have your hands full with this little minx, bud."

Tristan chuckled. "You can say that again. This was her bright idea."

"You're not going to hear me complain. I'm horny as hell." Shame walked over to where Sara sat on the foot of the bed. "So, what sinful ideas have you come up with for us?"

Sara's mind spun. This wasn't going to be as easy as she thought it would. In her mind, everything just happened. There was no discussion beforehand. Somehow, putting her desire into words was harder than actually doing it. "I want to see the two of you together."

Shame's eyes widened at her request but he didn't say no. The way his erection continued to grow under his pants told her he wasn't opposed to the idea.

Sara cast an uneasy glance at Tristan over Shame's shoulder. He nodded at her, urging her to get it all out. Sara took a deep breath. "After the two of you are done, I want the three of us to make love together." Inwardly wincing at her choice of words, Sara felt her face begin to heat again. *Make love*, how stupid was she? This was not going to be lovemaking. They were going to fuck, nothing more.

"Well." Shame grinned at her. "That sounds like a hell of a plan." He turned back to Tristan. "You okay with all of this, T?"

"Yeah, I'm good." Tristan didn't sound happy about it though. The clear outline of his full erection pressing against his pants said the exact opposite. If Sara thought for an instant that he wasn't interested, she wouldn't have asked. She wasn't about to let him go through something he didn't like just to make her happy.

"So how are we going to get this party started?" Shame faced Tristan, directing his question to him.

Tristan nodded toward Sara. "This is Sara's show. What happens next is up to her."

Both men looked at her, awaiting her instruction. Sara chewed on the inside of her lip, trying to think of how she wanted the tryst to play out.

"I want you to strip each other." Sara met Tristan's aquamarine eyes, read the heat behind them. "When you're naked I want you to rub your cocks together, touch each other, kiss…fuck. I want you to do it all, and I want you to let me watch."

Shame stood an arm's length away from Sara, the smooth, cut lines of his chest within touching distance. Tristan came up behind him. His muscular arms wrapped around Shame's waist, hands arrowing down to the snap on his jeans. He pulled them open, his long fingers slowly lowering the zipper, drawing the anticipation out. The jeans slid lower on Shame's hips but didn't drop as she longed for them to. Shame made an impatient noise in the back of his throat.

The sound made her nipples stand at attention. Sara wanted to yell at him to just do it, but she didn't. This wasn't about her. She was only a spectator.

Shame reached down to shove the offending garment off. His hands had barely touched the denim when Tristan grabbed his wrists, stilling him. "*Tsk, tsk.* Sara said we have to undress each other. That means you have to stand still and let me do it."

Shame growled. "Then get the hell on with it."

Tristan coughed back a laugh and pushed the denim over Shame's hips. The jeans hit the floor and Shame kicked them aside.

Sara's mouth gaped. Shame's penis was huge. Longer than Tristan's but not quite as thick. Plump, round balls, the color of smooth strawberry milk, were drawn up tight against the base of his cock. His groin was as hairless as his chest. Sara salivated. She wanted to touch all that smooth skin. Rub herself against the length of him like a cat.

"My turn," he said, turning to face Tristan, giving her a perfect bird's-eye view of his tight ass. Her fingers itched to slap the taut globes, watch them pinken under her hand. Shame stalked around Tristan, stopping behind him. Once there, he didn't waste any time getting rid of Tristan's pants. He quickly unbuttoned them and shoved them down and away.

Shame's head disappeared and Tristan groaned, low and ragged, at whatever Shame was doing to him. Tristan's already hard cock bobbed an inch higher and stayed there, pre-come oozing from the tip.

When Shame didn't reappear, Sara grew impatient. She wanted to see the action going on, not imagine it. She got up from the bed, circling around the men for a better view.

What she saw had her stomach muscles tightening. Blood rushed to fill her labia, engorging it around her clit, which distended hard and proud from beneath its hood. Liquid heat filled her pussy, rushed out to coat her lips in steamy anticipation.

Shame was bent over, his face buried between the firm cheeks of Tristan's rear. His flexible tongue foraged up and down through the separation, lingering over the puckered entrance to his rectum. Tristan moaned, long and deep. His back bowed as he leaned forward, bracing his weight on her bed's footboard.

Shame gave one last lingering lick. He pressed his tall form to Tristan's back and rubbed against him, his cock sliding through the wet groove he'd just been licking.

He reached around, fisting Tristan's cock, and vigorously pumped up and down. Perspiration popped out on Tristan's brow. Shame's back gleamed with sweat.

Sara didn't want to tear her gaze away but there was something missing. Something they needed. Walking backward, she hurried over to the nightstand. She searched until she found what she wanted; a bottle of lube and a condom.

Her nightgown and panties hit the floor as she made her way back over to them.

Sara offered Shame the condom and lube. He looked at the items in her hand, and then noticed her nakedness. His hot gaze moved over her slowly, from one end of her to the other, wiping away any doubts she'd had of whether or not he was attracted to women. He accepted the items, his fingers trailing over her hand as he took them. He murmured a gruff "Thanks" before turning his attention back to Tristan.

Legs trembling, Sara sat on the carpet beside them. She would've rather crawled up on the bed, but she wasn't willing to miss a moment of what they were doing. Not to mention the view wouldn't have been nearly as good.

Sara moaned, her gaze riveted on Shame's bare cock. So close, Sara could make out every ridge and vein of his thick shaft. She could also see that he had the same kind of penile tattoo Tristan sported. Before she could make out the tiny, navy lettering, Shame began to roll the thin latex over his dick. Shame's fingers curled around his prick, stroking slick lube up and down its length, and the curious tattoo was dismissed. She parted her saturated folds, her thumb zeroing in on her clit as he reached around to slather lube over Tristan's stiff erection.

Tristan's roughly growled, "Get on with it," had Shame chuckling as he lined the blunt head of his cock up with Tristan's ass, rubbing over the entrance once and then again. The pink, distended pucker seemed to flutter in anticipation right before Shame put the force of his body behind it and thrust home.

Shame moaned.

Tristan grunted, the muscles in his thighs standing out in tension.

One of Sara's hands squeezed and tugged at her swollen nipples, the other busily working her clit, driving her toward her own climax.

Shame pulled back, only the head of his cock remaining lodged inside Tristan, before forcing his way back in. Shame forged in and out, each stroke long and slow, dragging out the pleasure. His hand was fisted tightly around Tristan's penis.

With each plunge, he pumped his hand up and over the head, mimicking what he must have felt each time he entered his friend's asshole.

Both men panted, sweat rolling from their tense bodies. From the deep red tint of Tristan's cock, Sara knew it wouldn't be much longer before he came and pulled Shame over the edge with him. Determined to go with them, she rammed two fingers into her pussy, the heel of her hand grinding down on her clit.

Shame picked up his pace, slamming into Tristan. Sara watched his ass hollow out with every thrust. Heard the wet sound of their balls slapping together as Shame moved faster, his thrusts growing short and choppy.

She heard Tristan cry out, saw him jerk, come exploding from the head of his cock to cover Shame's fist, just as the first contraction inside her pussy sucked her fingers in deeper. Lost in the whirling cyclone of her own orgasm, Sara almost missed Shame's quiet growl of completion. She opened her eyes and saw the two men disengage, pulling away from each other. Shame turned his back, ridding himself of the used condom. Tristan slumped over the footboard.

Sara clumsily got to her feet and swayed drunkenly to the bed, falling back on it. The clitoral orgasm had been great, but couldn't compare to what Tristan did for her. It took the edge off the hunger caused by watching the men fuck, but it left her vaguely unsatisfied.

She wanted more.

Chapter Sixteen

Shame came out of the bathroom and plopped down beside her. The bed rattled, causing Tristan to finally raise his head. He pulled himself up and walked toward the room Shame had just left. Sara closed her eyes and replayed the torrid event she'd just witnessed.

As the images played on a constant loop, Sara felt herself growing wet again. Her breasts grew heavy, her nipples beading. Without thought her hand started the short pilgrimage to her sex. She stopped when she felt the bed shift beside her, reminding her she wasn't alone. Her hand flew back to her side.

Sara opened her eyes when she heard Shame chuckle. "I saw that, you bad girl. You really did get a boost out of watching us, didn't you?"

"Yeah. I guess I did."

"Mmm, good." Shame flipped onto his side, facing her. One long tapered finger ran up and down the inside of her arm. "I guess we get to play with you next, huh?"

"Do you want to?"

Shame shook his head at her. "Oh, now why would you want to ask me such a silly question? All you have to do is look down and you'll have your answer."

Sara glanced down. His erection loomed long and hard against his stomach, flushed a deep rose at the tip. "Can I ask you a question?"

"Sure."

"I couldn't help but notice earlier, that you have the same kind of tattoo on your, um, penis as Tristan. Is that some kind of kinky thing the two of you did together?"

"Shouldn't you ask Tristan about that?"

"I would, but he's so touchy about it. I don't want to do anything to make him uncomfortable. Things between us are good right now and I don't want to screw that up, but I'm curious about it."

"Mm, well, the marks are used like identifying markers. Something the lab scientists conjured up to set us apart from the main population. The letter stands for our first initial. The numbers, the order we were brought into the agency. T01 and S02."

Sara wrinkled her forehead. "Why there though? Seems like a dumb place to put something like that."

Shame laughed. "Who knows why they do anything. I guess they figured if they put them on our cock, we wouldn't be so keen on having it removed." Shame stroked his cock. "Personally, mine can stay there. I don't want needles anywhere near my junk."

Sara laughed, she'd never heard someone refer to their anatomy in quite that way. "Speaking of your *junk*." She blushed. "Do you, um, shave it?"

"Huh?"

"Do you shave your"—Sara pointed—"you know."

"My...you know? Sara, are you trying to ask me if I shave my groin?"

"Yes."

"No, I don't shave."

Sara stared at his groin in disbelief. "But you're so smooth."

"There's hair down there. You just have to get close enough to see it."

Sara was moving closer before she glanced up and caught the evil expression on his face. She smacked his thigh, laughing. "You're terrible."

"So my wife used to tell me."

Sara sat up. "You're married?"

"Yep."

"Um..." Sara wanted to ask if he was divorced or... She chewed her lip, trying to think how to phrase her question without sounding like an ass.

"No, she doesn't know I'm still alive. I guess technically, since I'm supposed to be dead and all, that makes our marriage null and void, doesn't it. Makes her a widow instead of my wife."

"Oh. I'm sorry." Sara didn't know what else to say.

Silence stretched, awkward and uncomfortable. Shame lay on his back beside her, his face turned away. The way his wide chest rose and fell, even and steady, made her think he was asleep but she couldn't be sure. He could've been playing possum, afraid she would ask more painful questions of him.

She was ready to crawl out of her skin by the time Tristan finally came swaggering back into the room, stark naked and yawning. He dropped down onto the bed and flung an arm over her waist, pulling her into his arms. Sara immediately curled into his embrace, wallowing in the feel of his hair-roughened body against hers. Being with Tristan felt so good—so right.

Twisting around, Sara faced him. She rubbed the rounded point of her nose against his, giving him Eskimo kisses. "I love you so much, Tristan."

Firm masculine lips crashed into hers, moving, grinding their mouths together. His kiss was brutal in its intensity, savage in its ability to break down her resistance. Sara panted, struggling to catch her breath.

Tristan pulled away, his own chest heaving under the exertion of his passion. Sara whimpered, protesting at the loss of contact. Softly brushing her hair away from her face, he stared deep into her eyes. "Sara...baby, love you...so damn much."

His lips ran fluttery kisses down the side of her neck and laved the tender skin below her ear. "Mmm..." he murmured against her skin. "Want you so bad...don't deserve you, princess."

Hot kisses and tender love bites had Sara's nipples aching in anticipation as he got closer and closer to them. His long tongue extended, hovering over one tight bud. Sara held her breath, waiting. When he didn't move she arched her back, lifting her breasts for him.

Tristan licked the underside of her breast. "Tristan...?"

"Hmm?" he asked with feigned innocence.

Sara sighed and arched her breasts higher, showing him what she wanted.

He skirted around her nipple, licking and nipping at the puckered flesh surrounding it. Sara groaned in frustration.

"What's the matter, baby? That wasn't what you wanted?"

Sara wanted to smack him for trying to be cute about it. "No, damn it!"

"Hmm." His eyebrows rose as he pretended to think on it. "How 'bout this?"

Tristan lowered his head, the raspy flat of his tongue swiping over her nipple. "Oh...yes!" Sara's eyelids lowered in pleasure. He laved one stiff nipple and then the other, switching back and forth. "More," she begged, wanting him to pull the nerve-enriched flesh into his mouth and suckle her.

A second, hot mouth covered her other nipple and sucked hard. Sara stiffened, her heavily lidded eyes opening. Shame's auburn curls at one breast, Tristan's dark locks at the other. Sara let her eyes fall back shut and went with it. What they were doing felt too damn good... Her fingers crept into each man's hair, holding them to her.

The men switched off, taking turns. One licked and teased while the other nipped and sucked. Gasping for air, Sara writhed under their delicious torment. Each tug on her nipple sent a streak of blazing heat to her core, making her melt.

Pressure built within her, her orgasm hovering just out of reach. She was so close. All she needed was one touch, some kind of direct stimulation and she would plummet right over the edge.

Sara let go of Shame's head. She wanted her hand free so she could rub her clit, make herself come. Traveling down over her ribs and the softly rounded expanse of her belly, she plunged two fingers though her wet folds and into her pussy. Drawing out moisture collecting there, she ran her fingers lightly over the swollen, blood-engorged lips and teased herself.

Tristan grabbed her wrists, drew them up over her head and pinned them there. "Ah, ah, ah. No touching. You'll come when we say so and not a minute before."

The thought of being at the mercy of two such powerful, sexy men kicked her desire up another notch. Sara struggled halfheartedly. "Damn it, Tristan, let me go."

Was she going to give up control? Hell yeah! If she submitted to them, gave them the power they wanted, all she had to do was lay back and enjoy the ride. She wouldn't have to worry about giving one of them more attention than the other, or what she looked like with her ass sticking up in the air. Handing over the reins to them meant sexual liberation for her.

That didn't mean she was going to lay back and go easy on them. Being stubborn and contrary meant her conscience wouldn't allow her to hand control over to them on a silver platter. If they wanted it, they were going to have to take it.

Shame let go of the nipple he was sucking, giving it one last flick with his tongue, before joining Tristan at the head of the bed.

Tristan lay to her right, his torso pressed against her, the hard ridge of his cock digging into her side. With one hand, he held her two above her head. The other he used to continue tormenting her, rolling and squeezing her aching nipples between his thumb and forefinger.

Shame sat to her left, his knees beneath him, the hard length of his penis in hand. He stroked up and down, his blunt fingers loosely massaging his engorged cock.

When he noticed her attention, a sexy smile tilted the corners of his full lips. "Like what you see, darlin'?"

Cheeky bastard. In return, Sara looked right at his cock, making an exaggerated show of licking her lips.

Shame groaned and glanced at Tristan. Silent communication passed between them before they turned their full attention back to her.

Shame inched closer, his hand once again pumping up and down his shaft. He loomed over her, the head of his cock brushing against her closed lips.

Musky arousal filled her nose. Made her want to stick her tongue out and lick him. Sara resisted temptation. She wanted to see where they were going with this before she did anything.

"Now, Sara," Shame said as he rubbed the wet tip of his cock over her lips. "Are you going to be good and do what we say? Or are we going to have to tie you down and make you behave?"

Her pulse thundered. This was it. She could back down if she wanted to, but what fun would that be? "Make me."

Both men groaned—long and ragged sounds that made Sara want to cream the sheets. Apparently they liked her choice. She had a feeling she was going to like it too.

Shame retreated, leaving the bed.

Tristan continued to lie alongside her. He pressed his lips lightly over hers, rubbing softly, enticing her to kiss him back. She couldn't resist, didn't want to. She pressed back, opening her mouth, letting his tongue slip through her teeth. Nimbly they played, foraging back and forth into each other's mouths, taking turns.

Tristan nipped her bottom lip. "Are you sure about this?" he whispered against her lips.

His concern for her touched Sara in ways nothing else could. "Yeah, I want to do this. I trust you not to do anything to hurt me."

He pulled back and looked down at her, a crease between his brows. "I would never intentionally hurt you, Sara."

"I know you wouldn't." Sara looked away.

Tristan caught her jaw, gently forcing her to face him. "I won't let anyone or anything hurt you again, baby. I promise. I never thought I would have the chance to be with you again. Now that I do, I'm sure as hell not going to let anything come between us. I'm going to stick so close to you and Sam that you get sick of having me around."

Sara laughed, her eyes filling with happy tears. "Never. I could never get sick of having you around. As soon as we let Sam know his daddy is home to stay, we're going to have one very excited little boy on our hands."

"Sara, I—"

"Look what I found." Shame sauntered up to the bed behind Tristan, a pair of her black silk stockings wrapped around his fist, interrupting whatever Tristan had been about to say.

He trailed the silk over Tristan's arm. "I think these will suit our needs just fine. What do you think, bro?"

Tristan glanced at him over his shoulder. "Those will do."

"Well, darlin', I think we're all set." He cocked one auburn eyebrow at her. "You ready?"

"Yep," Sara said. "Bring it on."

Shame opened his mouth to respond. Tristan cut him off. "Before we do anything—you need to pick a safe word, Sara. That way if anything happens that you don't like all you have to do is say the word and we'll stop."

"Okay." Sara thought for a moment. She smiled as the perfect word came to her. Why not? It wasn't like she was actually going to use it. There wasn't anything these two men could do to her that she wouldn't like. "I like the word *supercalifragilicous.*"

Shame laughed. "Hell of a word. You'd never say that one by accident." He handed the stockings over to Tristan. "Just keep in mind, Sara, if you say the safe word *everything* stops. So don't use it unless you really need to."

"I get it. Now how about the two of you put your money where your mouths are and get on with it." She smiled sweetly at Shame. "Unless you're all talk, no action."

"That sounds like a challenge," Tristan said, wrapping the hose snugly around each of her wrists and tying them around the thin wooden slats on her headboard.

"If that's what it takes." Sara dared both men to do their worst.

Tristan stuck his pointer finger between her skin and the hose, testing the restraints. "Are these okay? Not too tight?"

She moved her arms, testing them. There was very little play; she could scratch her nose but not much else. "They're fine, tight but not too uncomfortable."

Tristan snuggled up against her. "Good." He hugged her to him, his arm across her waist, his erection poking her in the side. He leaned over to kiss her and Sara strained up to meet his lips, eager to experience what most women only fantasized about.

Tristan dove right in, forcing his tongue into her mouth, pillaging its tender depths. Lost in the depth of the wet open-mouthed kiss, Sara didn't notice what Shame was doing until she felt the spongy tip of his cock brush against her and Tristan's fused lips. She broke the kiss, eager for a taste of him.

Sara licked her lips in anticipation. Groaned when Shame ignored her and forced the ruddy, flared crown into Tristan's mouth and allowed her to watch the action up close, in her face. Tristan's cheeks hollowed as he allowed more of his friend's cock to invade his mouth. Her womb clenched as

Tristan's eyes closed and a look of rapture appeared on his face, showing her how much he enjoyed pleasuring his partner.

Sara whimpered.

Tristan opened his eyes and met her gaze. Shame's flesh slipped from between his lips. Tristan grasped it around the base and guided it to her waiting mouth. The wide flare of Shame's cock crossed her lips, the broad crown rubbing over the flat of her tongue. Sara sucked him in deeper, taking him to the back of her throat, and swallowed as much of him as she could, wanting to please him as much as they were going to please her.

He felt like hot, living satin over steel. Tasted better than chocolate.

Shame pulled out almost as fast as he plunged in. "Shit. I can't take much of that. Not without giving one of you a mouthful."

"Wussy," Sara taunted him.

Tristan laughed, pinching one of her nipples. Sara's body went on autopilot, arching up into his touch. "We'll see who ends up begging. I don't think it will be either one of us, Sara."

Sara was too busy enjoying his touch to come up with a decent retort. Besides, he was probably right. It wouldn't take much from them before she started to beg. Begging for them fuck her, finish her off. She knew it and didn't care, but she'd be damned before she would admit it. "I haven't seen anything yet."

Swooping down, Tristan took her mouth in a savage kiss that stole her breath, made her pant. She lost herself in his touch, the mating of their mouths. Lips, teeth and tongues fought, mated and plundered. Sara shook. She couldn't get enough. She wanted more, always more.

She felt her legs being parted but couldn't see what was happening, couldn't force herself to end the kiss with Tristan to look. A hot, wet tongue plunged into her pussy. Sara shrieked into Tristan's mouth, her hips rising off the bed.

Shame ate her pussy, his long tongue lapping and sucking at her flesh, while Tristan did the same to her mouth. Both men forced their tongues in and out of her, licked and nipped at both set of lips, upper and lower. All Sara could do was take it and whimper from the pleasure they bestowed on her, her body straining toward an orgasm that shimmered just out of reach.

Fingers speared into her pussy, making her cry out as they stretched her to her limits, disappearing before she could adjust to them. Something wet and blunt tapped against the entrance to her backside and Sara tensed. Shame's finger circled her anus only for a second before going back to her pussy, plunging back inside again. Sara relaxed.

Rough calloused hands demanded her attention. Tristan's. He kneaded her breasts, massaging them one at a time, squeezing the firm mounds and pinching the hardened tips.

She couldn't concentrate, couldn't focus. Too many nerves were being stimulated at the same time, too many sensations racing through her body to keep track of each one. The walls of her pussy clenched and unclenched emptily, wanting something to grip, to fuck back against.

Shame's wet finger returned to prod at her anus. Sara didn't tense up, couldn't make her body cooperate. His finger forced its way through the tight ring of muscle guarding her anus and pushed deep inside. A second squeezed in alongside the first and twisted inside her passage, spreading her open. The small bite of pain intensified her pleasure.

Her own mindless whimpers filled the room as orgasm took her, washed over her in wave after wave, finally crashing her back into her skin. Her entire body shook, trembling from the power of her release.

The fingers ravaging her body disappeared. Tristan pulled his mouth away from hers and stared down at her.

Sara blinked up at him, wanting to beg him to take her but too hardheaded to say the words.

"Ready?" Tristan asked softly.

Sara nodded. "Fuck me. *Now.*"

Shame moved up to her side. She could feel him there but couldn't summon up enough spare energy to turn her head. Strong hands, Shame's, circled her wrists, untying the restraints, massaging the stiff muscles in her arms. He shifted her onto her side, facing away from him.

Tristan rolled onto his back beside her, his hard, thick cock full and ready, weeping against the taut skin of his abdomen.

Sara felt herself being lifted from behind. Shame picked her limp body up and laid her down on top of Tristan. Her legs automatically fell into position on either side of him. She wrapped her arms around Tristan's neck and kissed the hard collarbone resting under her cheek.

Tristan's rigid penis poked at the mouth of her vagina. Sara squirmed against him until she felt the tip of his cock enter. Hands around her waist prevented her from moving, from taking him any further inside her. "Patience, baby," Tristan murmured, his lips pressed to her forehead.

Shame settled in behind them, in the vee of Tristan's thighs and against her bottom. She felt hot, wet heat gliding over her asshole and moaned, her hips shifting restlessly.

Shame's tongue lapped at her, doing the same thing she'd watched him do to Tristan earlier. He licked and prodded her opening with his tongue, rimming her anus until she was once again moaning and whimpering with need.

Sara heard foil tearing. An instant later the sheathed end of his cock bumped against her. "Okay, Sara, here we go. I'm going to work my cock all the way into your tight little ass before Tristan takes your pussy. Take a deep breath and push out when I press in. It'll help."

Sara tensed up when the pressure against her anus intensified and began to burn.

"Relax, baby. You gotta relax or it's gonna hurt. Loosen up and let me in, baby."

Sara closed her eyes, took a deep breath and pushed out against him.

The wide head of his cock popped through her sphincter. Sara winced and bit her lip at the sharp, burning sting of his invasion. "Damn... So tight..." Shame cursed, groaning as he forced his way deeper, an inch at a time. "That's it, honey. Let me in... Gonna feel so good."

"Oh...*oh!*" The burning pressure in her ass started to morph into something that wasn't quite pain...not quite pleasure. More of an alien fullness that increased through the tight passage of her rectum as Shame shuttled in deeper, his cock bottoming out inside her.

With his groin pressed tight against her ass, Shame stilled. "I'm all the way in."

Sara started to reply, to tell him that she could have figured that out without having to be told, until she realized that he wasn't speaking to her.

Tristan cupped her chin and pressed a quick kiss to her lips. "Ready?"

Sara looked up into his face, his beautiful aquamarine eyes. She nodded. "Do it. I'm ready."

Tristan gripped her hips, steadying her. In one powerful upward thrust he surged to the hilt inside her.

Sara shrieked. "Oh God... Oh *my* God! Tristan."

And then she was beyond speech. Unable to do anything but feel as they surged into her. Tristan's thick cock barreling into her pussy as Shame eased out of her ass. Shame forcing his way back into her rectum, only the flared head of Tristan's cock remaining in her cunt.

Back and forth, faster and faster, in and out. Sara's head spun. Her ass burned, her pussy ached, her clit throbbed unattended. Small spasms chased each other through her cunt. *So close, so damn close.*

Shame's hands dug into her hips as he rammed the full length of his cock home inside her ass, bellowing as he came deep inside her. By slow increments, he worked his cock out of her bottom and then fell onto his back, spent.

Tristan surged up and rolled Sara to her back, kissing her breathless as he plunged his cock back inside her. Over and over he pounded into her pussy, riding her hard and fast. Showing her no mercy, he found her sweet spot and plowed into it with every thrust. "So good, Sara. You feel so damn good, baby. Gonna come so hard... Fill you full of my love... Make another baby."

Sara imploded, her release bursting over her so strongly that pinpricks of light splintered behind her closed eyelids. Oh God! She couldn't take it...it was too much...too good. Wildly, her head thrashed to and fro, hair whipping around her passion-flushed face. It went on and on, one strong contraction after another.

Tristan held her, his arms wrapped protectively around her until the last of the tremors passed and she finally collapsed, exhausted, against his chest.

Shame rolled up against her back, spooning her from the other side. She felt boneless and replete; unfortunately her sticky, sweaty body wasn't going to allow her to stay still for too long. She needed a shower in the worst way. The scent of their combined sweat and come mingled on her skin, making her itchy. There would be no more play and certainly no rest until she cleaned up.

But after the shower... Sara grinned at her own devious thoughts.

"Hey, I can feel that, you know."

Sara looked up at Tristan, batting her eyelashes innocently. "Feel what?"

"I can feel that evil little smile against my chest. What are you up to?"

Shame's hand snuck around her midsection and cupped her breast, kneading it. "I'm up for whatever the little darlin' has in mind."

Sara laughed and wiggled, Shame's renewed erection bumping up against her tailbone. He wasn't kidding when he claimed to be up for it. "Nothing." She smiled, her fingers playing in the dark hair between Tristan's nipples. "I was just thinking about how much I want a shower."

He cocked an eyebrow, his eyes lighting up sinfully. "A shower, huh? That could be fun."

"Mmm-hmm. A nice hot shower. Alone."

Tristan's head fell back to the bed. "Well there went that idea."

Shame groaned against her neck. "Spoilsport."

"Keep that thought." Sara's fingers stroked over his renewing erection. "I'll be back before you know it."

Sara scrambled from the bed. She stopped before she left the room, taking one more long look at both men lying naked on her bed. Her gaze crawled over Tristan's handsome face, stubbled jawline and the slight cleft in his chin. Over six feet of tanned muscle and sinew, all hers for the asking. She took a moment to appreciate his masculine beauty. The firm pecs, ridged abdomen, long lean legs. What lay between them. His penis twitched, feeling her intense perusal. Yummy.

Her gaze moved to Shame, who winked at her and spread his legs. He cupped his balls, his other hand moving down over his flat stomach to grip the base of his semi-hard cock and wag it at her.

Laughing, she exited the room. Jumping back into bed with them sounded divine, but a hot shower was in order first.

Chapter Seventeen

Sara rinsed the foamy lather from her hair with a contented sigh. Nothing felt better than a clean body. Of course, getting it dirty had felt pretty damn incredible too.

She smiled at the stupid thought, too giddy to control herself. Tristan loved her, wanted to marry her. It wasn't possible to be happier than she was at that moment.

Sara picked up a can of shaving cream, shook it, and sprayed a great big dollop into her palm. A quick touchup and she would be ready to get out. She couldn't get back to bed fast enough, not when two gorgeous men awaited her.

As she finished spreading the whipped mixture over her legs, Sara wondered if they'd be up for another round. She was pleasantly sore from the first one, but not enough to keep her from doing it again if she could talk them into it. She reached for a razor, her fingers fumbling with it, when darkness engulfed her. The razor slipped from the shelf, hitting the bottom of the tub with a muffled rattle.

Blindly, Sara's hands felt around her. Damn it! Not again. She followed the wall, trying to keep her balance as she sank to the tub floor. Water cascaded over her immobile body.

When her vision began to clear, she saw darkness and a single light off in the distance. As the light grew closer, Sara could make out more of her surroundings. She was in a hallway, moving toward an open door at the end of it.

She entered a dimly lit room, strange devices lining the cement walls. She had no idea what the names of the apparatuses were, but their use was apparent. Torture.

Her tunnel vision panned out, allowing her to see more. She belatedly wished it hadn't. A young woman with blonde hair was strapped to a big metal X in the middle of the room. Blood oozed from her wrists and ankles where she was bound to the structure by cuffs of barbed wire. What little Sara could see of her back and outer thighs was covered in wide, red welts.

Sara didn't know what could have caused the marks and she didn't want to find out. She didn't want to see any more. Couldn't take seeing another person die and not being able to do anything to stop it.

The vampire began to move around the woman. He was so close Sara could hear the woman whimpering, see the sobs that shook her slender frame. Her body stiffened and Sara knew the woman had finally heard the creature approaching.

"Please," the woman begged, her voice hoarse and thick with emotion. "Don't hurt me any more. I'll do whatever you want. Just don't hurt me."

Sara's heart stopped in mid-beat. She knew that voice. *Please, no.* Sara prayed she was wrong. That it wasn't...

A misshapen clawed hand lifted within Sara's line of sight, one black, arrowed nail scraping down the back of the woman's thin arm, drawing a crimson line of blood from her skin. She shrieked, the sound of her pain echoing through the room.

Sick at heart, Sara watched, unable to look away.

The vampire moved in front of the woman, revealing her face. The blonde up on the torture rack was Cindy.

In horror, Sara looked her friend over. Her front was worse than her back. Black rings circled both of her bloodshot eyes. Thin, bloody scratches covered both cheeks. A raw, puckered wound marred one side of her swanlike neck. Small circular burn marks littered her chest, including one nipple. Dried blood smeared down the inside of her thighs.

Sara's heart broke for her friend.

A loud voice boomed through Sara's ears. "Speak." She recognized it as belonging to the creature that attacked her.

Cindy flinched, her body visibly shaking in fear. "Please," she begged, her gaze staring right into the vampires, and in essence, Sara's as well. "Please, Sara, you have to help me."

Sara couldn't make out the next few words. Cindy sobbed so hard her words came out slurred and incomprehensible. Her bruised chest rose and fell, her respiration short and choppy. Just as she was breaking into full hyperventilation the beast seemed to lose his patience with her and smashed his open palm into the side of her face. His hand flashed by so quickly Sara would have missed it, had she the ability to blink.

Cindy's head fell to one side, blood trickling from the corner of her lip. Short, gasping breaths were the only sound she made.

A long, black, leather whip snapped at the ground around Cindy's feet. The sound of it ricocheted like a gunshot through the closed room. "Say it, bitch, or I'll flay the skin from your back."

Cindy's head snapped up, her eyes wide as saucers. "Please don't. Oh, God! No more. I'll do it. I'll do whatever you say, just no more." She looked directly at Sara, her heart in her eyes. "Sara, you have to come. You have to help me. He says he'll kill me if you don't. He...he...he says he'll go after Sam when he's through with me. You have to come here, 125 Ridgemont Drive. Tonight. Alone."

The whip cracked against her calf, splitting the skin, leaving the flesh beneath raw and bleeding. "*Ow.*" Cindy screamed, recoiling back as far as she was able while bound. "Please God! Sara...he says he'll know if you aren't alone."

Sara's vision winked out. Her friend's pleading voice was the last thing she heard.

Slowly Sara's senses came back to her. She was sitting in a pool of icy water in the bottom of the bathtub. Her entire body was crinkled up like a prune. Goose bumps covered her from head to toe.

Shivering, Sara turned off the water, her teeth rattling.

She had to do something. Save Cindy. Protect Sam. But how?

She couldn't tell the men. The vampire insisted she come alone. Trade her life for Cindy's...and in essence Sam's. She was the one the vampire wanted. If she sacrificed herself, Sam would be safe. If she didn't, all three of them were as good as dead. Because of her connection to him, they couldn't hide from the monster. He would find them wherever they went. Hunt them, until they had nowhere left to go. There had to be a way out. Something she could do without committing virtual suicide in the process.

Think, Sara, think.

As the fog over the bathroom mirror cleared, and Sara's reflection stared back at her contemptuously, she began to form a plan.

Tristan woke in layers. He slowly grew aware of his surroundings; gauzy morning light filtering through the sheer mauve curtains, warm cotton sheets rubbing sensuously against his bare skin, delicious heat from the soft body behind him.

Sara.

Images of the night before unfolded in his mind. God, he thought the top of his head was going to come off by the time he finally let himself go and came long and hard inside her. She'd given him the best damn orgasm of his life.

He must have fallen asleep right afterwards. He remembered holding her, rocking her in his arms while her climax waned. Her getting up to take a shower afterwards. Nothing following that registered.

His morning wood grew stiffer, a little more insistent. Thinking a good round of sweaty morning sex was just what the doctor ordered, he rolled over to wake Sara up with a good-morning kiss.

She wasn't behind him. Shame was.

Damn! There went his morning sex. Sara must have gotten up with Sam. The boy was probably already up and running circles around the house, the same as every other morning. Having a kid in the house was going to take some getting used to, but he looked forward to it.

Tristan climbed out of bed, careful not wake Shame. The man could be a testy little bitch if he was woken up too early. Walking across the room, he found the jeans he'd discarded the night before still laying in a crumpled pile on the floor and yanked them up his legs. They were wrinkled and stiff, but he couldn't very well go running around the house naked with his kid around.

Tristan shook his head. His kid. It still amazed the piss out of him.

Absently, he wondered when he and Sara would be able to sit down with Sam and tell him that he was his dad. Probably not until he and Shame had taken care of the threat to her and he was free and clear of the SCS, at least. Anxious to tell his son the truth, it gave him yet another reason to hurry and win his freedom. He wanted to start building the father/son relationship he'd always envisioned having with his children.

He'd lost so much time with Sam. The first five years of his life were a blank void in Tristan's mind. He'd missed all the important firsts—first tooth, first word, first step. He didn't intend to miss out on anything else. The house was deathly quiet as he made his way down the hall to the stairs. The only sound he heard was his muffled footsteps on the thick blue carpet. While the complete lack of sound concerned him, he figured he was only being paranoid and pushed down the uneasy feeling in his gut.

He walked through the living room, heading for the eat-in kitchen. Sara probably hadn't been up for long and was just fixing breakfast for Sam. That would explain why they were so quiet. They weren't fully awake yet.

The kitchen was empty.

His gut twisted. Something wasn't right. Where was everyone?

Maybe they were out in the backyard...

Tristan turned to leave the room. He stilled as an envelope with his name written boldly across the front of it caught his attention. A yellow smiley-face magnet held it in place on the refrigerator door.

Palms damp with nervous sweat, Tristan snatched it off the fridge and tore it open. Sara's flowery script filled the single sheet of notebook paper. Gut clenching in abject misery, he read...

Tristan,

Words cannot express the joy I've felt having you back in my life. I'm sorry that I have to leave and place myself in harm's way but there's no other option.

While I was in the shower, I was hit by another one of the visions you predicted. Only this time it was worse. So, so much worse, because this time it's personal. Tristan, he has Cindy.

I was told to come alone to the address I was given. I'm sorry I couldn't confide in you, but we both know you never would've let me go in alone. I couldn't risk not following the directions. There is more in jeopardy than just myself now. It's my fault that Cindy's there. My fault Sam's in danger. I alone can ensure Cindy's release and Sam's future.

Even knowing I may fail...I have to try.

I know that if something goes wrong and I don't make it back, I can count on you to raise our son with all the love and care I want for him.

Remember,

I love you,

Sara

Drywall cracked and separated around his closed fist as it tore into the wall. The slow ache of his bloodied knuckles helped him feel something other than the helpless, bilious terror he felt worming its way through his system.

How could Sara be so damn naive? She'd walked her pretty ass right into a trap.

Tristan ran back up the stairs screaming for Shame to wake up. He needed to get Sam up and find somewhere safe to stash him while they were gone. Then he was faced with the prospect of coming up with a plan to rescue Sara.

୨୦୧୫

Sara felt like a goddamn idiot. She'd fled the safety of her house and the two men protecting her, planning to storm into the creature's house with a pistol she had no idea how to even use, and demand Cindy's release, somehow kill the beast and walk right back out unscathed.

Who the hell had she been kidding?

What she got was a blast to the back of the head as soon as the arched front door swung open. By the time she'd come to she found herself in some kind of medieval-looking dungeon.

Except for the dirty, bloodstained twin mattress in one corner, the room was bare. The floor, walls and ceiling were formed by cement. A small, barred window the size of a hardback novel allowed in a minute amount of dingy light.

Sara walked the perimeter of the room. The chain around her ankle clanked with each step. A metal "O" ring in the middle of the cement floor anchored the chain, assuring she couldn't go far. A cruel reminder of her inability to escape the torment the creature had in store for her.

The worst thing was being alone. She'd seen no trace of Cindy, nor had she heard anything. The room was silent as a tomb. It was beginning to feel like one as well.

How could she have been so damn stupid? She felt like the insipid heroine from a horror movie, the one everyone screamed at for being a dumbass. God, what had she gotten herself into?

Sara clung to the anger racing through her veins. At the moment it was all she had. If not for it, she knew she would dissolve into a crumpled mass of terrified gelatin on the cold cement.

ঔওত্ত

Tristan sat with his elbows on his knees, his face resting in his hands. The waiting was killing him. He knew they couldn't afford to make any mistakes, couldn't go in guns a-blazing like in some pulp novel, but that was exactly what his instincts screamed out at him to do.

His emotions running high, Tristan had managed to cajole Mark into staying with Sam. Afterward, he and Shame, with the help of John Ramsey, spent the better part of the afternoon devising a plan to rescue Sara. John was adamant about now being the time to implement his goals to achieve their independence into the mix, which sucked away a huge chunk of time Tristan didn't want to spare, but had little choice in changing.

He knew they needed the cover of darkness for either plan to work, but it was all he could do to wait, instead of running to Sara as fast as his legs would carry him. Thanks to the GPS he'd installed on her car and Shame's scouting, they already knew where she was, it was just a matter of going to her. Tristan's mind was consumed with it, leaving him unable to think about his own freedom or that of Shame's, his only concern focused on the woman he loved and the danger she faced.

He knew The Mangler wouldn't kill Sara. If he'd wanted her dead, he would have finished her off in the woods, instead of allowing her wounds to heal. However, that didn't mean he wouldn't torture or rape her, break her spirit until she gave up hope and cooperated enough to allow him to start the long and painful process of turning her into a vampire, like him.

Sweet Jesus, Tristan wasn't sure he could wait another minute. The wondering, the incessant worry, was eating him alive, rapidly dissolving his resolve to stick with their plan. They were trained to stay unattached, so that their instincts weren't swayed by their emotions. Involving his emotions was stupid, and had the potential to be disastrous, but how could he do anything else? It was his woman out there, alone and afraid.

He watched the clock, the seconds ticking by ever so slowly, and waited for the moment they could make their move.

Chapter Eighteen

Shadows crept across the floor, drawing closer to where Sara's feet rested on the edge of the stained mattress. As the sun descended lower in the sky it took with it what little light illuminated her temporary prison.

Sara knew with one hundred percent certainty that sooner or later she would be freed from the small enclosure she'd spent the day in. What bothered her was how she would be leaving and what would happen to her once she was out.

Her mind spun, frantic to drudge up all the details about vampires she'd learned from watching television and seldom-read horror novels. The best she came up with was crosses, wooden stakes and holy water. Fat lot of good that would do her since she didn't have any of those things in her pockets at the moment.

She'd cursed herself all day for not asking more questions. Why hadn't she picked Shame and Tristan's brain for more information about the beast after her?

Sara knew why. She'd been too busy with her head up her butt, worrying about all the drama swirling around her relationship with Tristan, or lack thereof, to concentrate on the things she should've been most worried about. Namely the damned vampire and what she had to do to kill it.

A scuttling noise sounded on the other side of the door. Sara jerked her head up, her heart pounding in trepidation. All her attention focused on the thick wood as the sound of a metallic click registered. *A key?* Was someone unlocking it?

Timed slowed to a crawl as she watched the brass doorknob slowly begin to rotate.

Sara held her breath...waiting.

On a loud creak, the door swung inward. Bright light silhouetted the person standing in the open doorway.

"Sweet, sweet, Sara."

Sara gasped, tears streaming down her soiled face.

Cindy stood outlined in the doorway. What skin wasn't covered by the black turtleneck and indigo blue jeans she wore was riddle with scratches and smears of dried blood, but she was alive and that was all that mattered.

Sara ran to Cindy, forgetting about the chain around her ankle until it yanked her backward, stopping her a few feet short of being able to embrace her friend. "Cindy...thank God. I was so worried about you. So sacred that he'd...that he'd..."

Cindy took a step farther into the room. Only then did Sara sense a difference in her friend. She looked the same, but the air, the very aura surrounding her was changed, somehow altered. Darker.

Stumbling back, Sara tripped over her own two feet and hit the hard cement floor on her ass.

"Sweet Sara, how gullible you are." Cindy's voice was calm, mellow. Almost seductive in its new husky tenor. "The Master said you would come running to rescue me, but I didn't really believe you would be that stupid. You didn't even notice the welts healing on my skin right before your eyes." She laughed. "Did you really think that the Master would still want a fat little frump like you when he could have something like *this*?" Cindy's long, tapered fingers swept down over her small breasts and the indentation of her waist, stopping at the slight flare of her hips.

Who was this crazy bitch? And what had she done with the real Cindy?

"Cindy...?"

Cindy advanced toward her. "Nope. Save it, toots. I don't want to hear your wretched whining. I've had to listen to you drone on and on about your pathetic excuse for a life way too long as it is. Whatever you have to say can be said directly to the Master. If he decides to grace you with a visit. He's much too important and busy to waste his time on a sniveling little bitch like you."

On her hind end and hands, Sara scrambled backward. For every foot of space she put between them, Cindy came forward another two. Her back hit the wall. There was nowhere else to go. She was trapped.

Cindy towered over her, a smirk twisting the corners of her plump red lips. "I came to deliver you a warning. The Master belongs to me now. If I so much as catch you batting your trampy eyelashes at him, I won't hesitate to cut off your head and shit down your neck." She shoved a pointed fingernail under Sara's chin and twisted it against the rapid pulse beating there. "Get me?"

Sara's nod was so slight it was almost unperceivable. She was afraid to move her head much on account of the sharp nail poking into her jugular. She tried to tell herself that this was Cindy, her best friend. The only person who had stuck by her through all the laughter and tears in her life. The only real friend she had. Cindy wouldn't hurt her. Couldn't.

All it took to disprove that theory was one deep look into the "new" Cindy's wild, bloodshot eyes. This was not the same person who'd been her friend since junior high. If she wanted to live, Sara was going to have to keep reminding herself of that.

The nail pressing into her throat retreated. Sara gulped in a deep breath of life-giving oxygen. Anger exploded inside her. *Fuck this.* She pushed up and out, shoving Cindy roughly away from her. Jumping to her feet, Sara pounced.

They circled each other warily. She saw Cindy's eyes widen a fraction before she struck out. Sara raised her arm, blocking the blow.

Back and forth they fought, Sara gaining ground merely to lose it when Cindy advanced on her yet again. Only the random spurts of pain in her body grounded Sara in reality, reminding her that this was real and not just another horrific nightmare.

A particularly sharp slap to the back of the head had Sara's ears ringing, her stomach churning. Dizzily, she kicked out, her foot hitting Cindy's shin.

Sara could no longer delude herself into thinking even the smallest portion of her friend existed inside the vicious bitch before her. This fight was to the death, kill or be killed, and Sara knew it.

Sara struck out with her right fist, slamming it into the under bridge of Cindy's nose and shoved upward. She heard cartilage snap and felt the hot gush of blood against her palm. Kicking out with her left leg, Sara knocked Cindy down.

Sara pounced on Cindy's back and ground her face into the unyielding cement. Cindy squealed at the impact to her broken nose.

"Where's the fuckin' key to the shackles?"

No answer. Gripping a handful of pale blonde hair, Sara yanked Cindy's head up and shoved it back down into the cement as hard as she could.

Cindy howled.

"I'm only going to ask you one more time. Where's the goddamn key?"

"This what you're looking for?"

The loud voice coming from behind her made Sara forget about the woman beneath her. Her head shot up and around.

"Surprised to see me?"

Speechless, Sara stared at Lester Morgan, her boss. He stood stark naked, his emaciated frame casually leaning against the doorframe. One hand was propped on his hip, the other held out the key to her restraints.

She blinked. *What the hell?*

Sara's grip faltered.

Cindy surged up, bucking Sara off her back. "You're gonna pay for breaking my nose, bitch!"

Sara's ass hit the cold concrete with a thud. In a flash of movement too fast for Sara to clearly make out, Cindy was squatting over her. Blood pooled beneath her nose and dripped from her chin. An evil grin slowly spread across her face.

As Sara watched, disbelief and terror coursing through her veins, a second razor-sharp set of serrated teeth popped through Cindy's gums and covered the human-looking pair. Cindy moved forward, the fetid stench of her breath blowing over Sara's face. Recoiling, Sara's head hit the wall behind her with a loud thunk. Pain exploded behind her eyes.

The sun chose that precise moment to finish setting, plunging the room into complete darkness.

Cindy laughed. The hollow sound echoed through the room. "Aw, poor *wittle* Sara's scared. You aren't worried about what I intend to do you with my pretty new teeth are you, Sara?"

Anger overrode Sara's caution. "Do it then," she demanded. "If you're going to kill me, then do it!" Sara reached out blindly and shoved against Cindy's collarbone. She didn't budge an inch. "Quit fuckin' toying with me and get on with it."

Cindy leaned in closer, the slimy tip of her tongue swiping Sara's jaw. "Is that the best you've got? And here I thought I might actually get to have a little fun with you, maybe even put on a nice show for Master, before I finished you off. Guess I was wrong."

The sharp edge of teeth pressed into her neck.

In a blink, Morgan loomed over them. "No! She's mine!" His clawed fists sank into Cindy's shoulders, ripping through skin and muscle, severing one side of her neck from her body. Sara screamed as blood spewed over her face. Morgan slung Cindy's limp body across the room. She hit the wall with a sickening thud before landing on the floor in a puddle of her own blood.

In a flurry of motion that made Sara's head spin, Morgan lifted her into the air and shoved her up against the hard, damp wall. Sara kicked out at him, aiming for his drooping balls. "Goddamn you, let me go!"

Trapping her legs on either side of him, Morgan's cadaverous naked body pressed into her, holding her in place. "Do you actually think I'd let you go now that I finally have you?" He shook her, banging her head into the wall. "Foolish girl, don't you realize that everything I've done has been for you?" He cackled. "As soon as you entered my office, I knew you were the woman I wanted. All these years I've waited, fearing you would never appear, and then there you were, applying for a job. You came to me.

"For the last ten months I patiently bided my time, allowing you to get to know me at work. The murders, the visions, all of it was to prepare you for being mine. I was even thoughtful enough to transform your friend, so she could help see you through the transition, ungrateful bitch though she turned out to be." He made a derisive noise in the back of his throat. "Nevertheless, you've made me wait long enough. It's time to take your rightful place by my side. This is where you belong, Sara. Under my hand, forced to submit to me. Once I fuck you, mark you as mine, you'll know I speak the truth."

Razor-sharp talons slithered between them to rip and tear at her clothing. Unable to move, Sara cried, helpless tears streaming down over her cheeks.

The putrid stench of decay filled her pores, burned into the cavity of her nose. Bile rose in her throat as the tip of his thin cock prodded her, trying to gain entrance to her body. Sara braced herself for the assault. There wasn't a damn thing she could do to stop him.

ಬಂಡ

Outside, Shame detonated the second bomb right on the heels of the first. Tristan watched in horror as the house's structure trembled and began to collapse in on itself. The explosions they'd planned to use as a diversion were too powerful. The building was falling apart under the strain, sections of the further-out wings already beginning to cave.

Somewhere inside, Sara was in danger. His brain screamed in agony. Tristan left Shame behind, squatting in the bushes, and sprinted across the lawn. He didn't slow as he approached a large picture window, only raised his rifle and fired. It exploded in a hail of glass that peppered Tristan's face and neck as he took a running leap through the jagged opening.

Tristan hit the ground rolling, his gun safely held above his head. Smoke and dust littered the air, making it hard to breathe as he traversed one hallway after another, screaming Sara's name. He prayed with fervor, begging God to let him find Sara in time. Without her, he had no reason to go on.

ಐಌ

A loud blast from somewhere within the building echoed through the silence. Tall flames lit up the nighttime sky, briefly illuminating the room.

Penis poised at the mouth of her vagina, Morgan froze, cursing. Another explosion shook the house. This one closer. The walls around them shook. Sara shrieked as debris fell all around them. A large piece of the ceiling right above them caved in, knocking Morgan from his feet. Chunks of heavy cement landed atop him, smashing into his head and torso with deadly accuracy.

Another chunk fell, glancing off Sara's shoulder. She screamed, her arms flying up to protect her head as more cement crashed to the floor. In a desperate bid to save her hide, Sara crawled on her hands and knees until she felt the cushy material of the mattress under her fingers. With shaky hands, she pulled and tugged, fought with the damn thing until she got it situated over her upper body.

Sara curled up into a fetal ball and prayed, the loud thunder of her own heartbeat and the house collapsing around her the only noise she heard.

The sound of her name being screamed caused Sara to flinch, trying to crawl deeper under the mattress. She knew it was useless. The creatures knew where to find her. She was chained to the floor, it wasn't like she was going anywhere.

As the screaming grew louder, Sara began to think her mind was playing tricks on her. The voice sounded an awfully lot like Tristan but she knew that couldn't be. Tristan had no idea where she was. Hell, she wasn't sure where she was. The chance of him being able to find her was slim to none.

The owner of the voice was in the room with her, standing damn near on top of her. She could hear the footsteps, hear the man kicking debris out of his way as he walked. "Sara! Where are you? If you can hear me, say something, make a noise. *Please.* Sara!"

Oh my God! It was Tristan. She was sure of it.

"Tristan!" she shouted, her voice muffled under pounds of padding. "Tristan, I'm here!" She pushed and shoved, trying to get out from under the mattress. "I'm under here!"

She heard clanking and the loud crumbly sound of cement bricks hitting each other and smashing. The foam over her was yanked away, revealing the scratched and bloody face of the man she loved. Sara stared up into his pale blue eyes so full of love, worry and relief and promptly burst into tears.

Tristan pulled off his T-shirt and covered her nakedness, gently guiding her head and arms through the holes. "Sara, baby, don't cry. It's okay." Hard muscular arms swooped down beneath her, lifting her from the rubble. "I'm here now, baby. Everything's going to be okay." He turned and started out of the room.

"Tristan, the chain…"

He looked down, only then seeing the shackle around her ankle. "Hold on." He raised the mean-looking rifle he carried and took aim. "Cover your ears, baby."

Sara did as he said, her hands covering her ears tightly a second before the loud blast fired through the room, echoing as it hit and decimated the chain. The ankle cuff and a small length of the steel chain remained on her leg but it was no longer connected to anything.

Wrapping her arms around his neck, Sara hung on to him. She buried her face in the curve of his shoulder and let the sobs come. They shook her body, one after another. She gasped in deep breaths of smoke-filled air, trying to calm herself. "How...how did you find me?" she asked when she regained enough of her composure to think clearly.

Tristan remained silent. It wasn't until they were outside, a good distance from the house, that he chose to answer her. He looked down at her, a crease between his eyebrows and a flame of anger burning brightly behind his dark eyes. "The GPS on your car."

Sara looked away. Took in all the destruction around them. The house was on fire. One entire wing was nothing more than crumpled stone. Sirens in the distance grew louder as they neared the house. "Oh."

"*Oh*? That's all you have to say? What the hell were you thinking, running off by yourself like that? You could've been killed. You're damn lucky you weren't."

"I'm sorry, Tristan. I had to try. Cindy—"

"I know," he interrupted. "Shame came in behind me. He's still inside. I have to go back—"

Fire engines pulled up in front of the house. Loud sirens drowned out the sound of her voice. Firemen began to swarm the house, long hoses blasting water at the burning building.

Tristan said something she couldn't make out. He handed her off to the first fireman who approached and turned, heading back toward the house.

The line of firefighters spraying down the building yelled out to him. Tried to stop him from going back in. One made a grab for him, that Tristan deftly sidestepped. He ignored them and continued on, determined to get back inside and help his friend.

Sara broke free of the man holding her and ran across the yard after him. "No, Tristan, wait! You can't... You don't understand! Cindy's a—"

An explosion inside the house rocked the earth beneath her feet. Sara fell face forward onto the cold ground. She looked up just as the last few remaining walls caught fire and collapsed inward.

A loud animalistic wail filled the air. It wasn't until hard arms picked her up from the ground and she looked into the eyes of her father, that she realized the noise came from her.

Chapter Nineteen

Rain poured from the overcast sky as Sara watched an oak casket covered with white roses being lowered into the ground. Her fingers tightened around the umbrella she held, tears streaming down her cheeks. For the second time, she was forced to watch as the man she loved was lowered into the earth.

As the minister finished his speech, Sara bent down and grasped a handful of dirt. Mark stood beside her and held her hand as they walked to the graveside's edge. She dropped the required earth into the grave, bowed her head to say her final goodbyes and turned away in silence.

She left her hand in Mark's as they walked through the graveyard, back toward the parking lot and his waiting car. Mark held the passenger-side door open for her and Sara numbly slid inside. She stared out the window, the lush greenery a blur before her eyes, as he drove her home.

Shortly thereafter, Mark pulled into her driveway and threw the car into park. He looked at her over the console. "Are you sure you're doing the right thing?"

Sara eyed her loaded-down car, the trailer attached to the back with everything she owned carefully packed away inside. While apprehensive about the decision to move halfway across the country, she knew it was for the best. She and Sam could begin a new life, somewhere without painful memories etched on every sidewalk. "Yes, I'm sure. We've already talked about this, Mark. We'll be fine. And we'll keep in touch. You know that."

After the smoke had cleared away and the bodies were recovered, there were too many people left speculating about what had really happened inside Lester Morgan's mansion that night. Her father had been an odd source of support in the days that followed, actually having been the one to suggest the move in the first place. Theirs would never be a close relationship, there was too much hurt and water under the bridge for that, but it was amicable and that was good enough for her. Ramsey had even spoke of buying a place near wherever they ended up, saying he wouldn't mind staying close, getting to know his grandson.

Mark sighed. "Yeah, I guess I do. I'll miss you guys though." He leaned across the seat, pressing a chaste kiss to her forehead. "Make sure you call as soon as you get there. First thing, okay?"

"I will, I promise. Now I have to go. I still have a million things to do before we can leave."

Mark grasped her hand, squeezing it tightly before letting go. "Drive safely."

"I will, Mark." She paused, just then remembering the ring she'd slipped into her pocket that morning. She retrieved it, glancing down at the way it sparkled and caught the light, before sliding it onto the console toward Mark. "I'm sorry things didn't work out differently for us, but…" She trailed off, not sure what to say. "You take care of yourself."

Sara got out of the car and stood on the curb, watching while Mark backed out and drove away.

Entering the house, Sara spied Sam sitting on the floor, playing a handheld video game. Absorbed in whatever game he played, Sam didn't look up until she stood over him, her shadow blocking his light. "Hey, Mom," he said, dismissing her when his attention went right back to his toy.

"Hey yourself, champ. You about ready to hit the road?"

He looked back up at her, annoyance written on his face at her repeated interruption. "Yeah."

"You stay right here. I'll be back in a minute and then we're going to go. I don't want to have to come looking for you." Sara started to turn away and then remembered something else. "You should go outside and walk Bob before we leave. It's a long drive and I'd rather him not have any little accidents in the car."

Sam set down his video game. "Okay."

Sara watched her son trudge down the basement stairs to get Bob before turning her attention back to the house. She wanted to give it one last look-over before she left. They'd made a lot of good memories here. A lot of bad ones as well. Those she would just as soon forget.

She heard the back door slam shut before she trudged up the stairs. She entered her bedroom, now bare, only the plush mauve carpet and wallpaper left to speak of her presence there. Yep, she would miss the old house. It had been a good home for her and Sam while it lasted.

An arm shot out from behind her and wrapped around her, yanking her back against a broad, masculine chest. "What took you so long?"

Sara craned her neck, staring up into an identical set of aquamarine eyes that gazed out at her from her son's face. She shrugged. "It's not easy burying the man you love."

One dark eyebrow rose. "Well, if you take into consideration that Sam and I have been right here in the house waiting for you to come home, I wouldn't think it would be too hard on you."

Sara groaned. "Don't remind me. Besides, I couldn't very well act suspicious and give away that you aren't really dead, now could I?"

Tristan nipped at her neck, directly beneath her ear. "No, but you didn't have to spend so much time there. I missed you."

"What would you've had me do—dance a jig on the empty casket? That wouldn't have been very convincing if your former employer sent someone to watch like Ramsey suspected they would."

Tristan rubbed his nose against the side of her face. Kissed her cheek. "Did you see anyone who looked out of place?"

"No, but then I wasn't searching the crowd either. I was too busy trying to stay in character. I'm afraid you're not getting much of an actress. If anyone was watching, I hope they bought the act."

"I'm sure you did fine." Tristan spun her around and gazed down into her eyes. "We've nothing to worry about. It's all smooth sailing from here on out for us."

Tristan pressed his lips to hers, kissing her softly, sweetly. Sara twined her arms around him and hugged him tight. She broke the kiss, before she began to melt in his arms like chocolate on a hot summer day. They had a long drive ahead of them and needed to be on their way. There would always be time to make love later. A new home awaited them and she intended to christen every room.

Tristan stared down at her, a serious expression on his handsome face. "Have I told you how much I love you today?"

"Only about a hundred times but I wouldn't mind hearing it again."

"I love you, Sara McCoy. You know we still haven't figured out what my new name's going to be. What would you say to being Mrs. Stan McCoy? We'll keep your last name since we obviously can't use mine. That way you won't have to change either yours or Sam's last name."

"Sounds good to me, *Stan*. Just don't get mad at me if I yell out the wrong name during sex."

"We'll just have to keep practicing until you get it right."

The grin that spread across Sara's face was filled with wicked delight. "Well, you know what they say—practice makes perfect."

Epilogue

Heavy boot pressed down over the accelerator, Shame sent the souped-up sedan he drove soaring down the interstate. He felt a little bad for leaving Sara and Tristan to deal with the backlash from the explosion, but not enough to stay. He'd made sure they wouldn't have to worry about Lester Morgan anymore, at least.

Trapped under the rubble, his body twisted and broken, Morgan had still been clinging to life when Shame entered the room to double-check behind Tristan. Shame had known his partner's first concern was Sara and he hadn't wanted to leave anything to chance. As far as Shame was concerned, the jagged chuck of cement he'd used to finish severing Morgan's head from his body had been too quick a death for the vicious bastard. He would've liked drag it out and make the son of a bitch suffer, but there wasn't time. He'd barely managed to plant the cadavers Ramsey had altered to match his and Tristan's dental records and sneak out through the back, before the final explosion.

A good tune came on the radio and Shame bent forward to turn it up. Adrenaline coursed through his veins, making his heart race and his body sweat. He was excited, but also as nervous as a virgin at prom.

Over six long years had passed since he'd been home. Considering that everyone he loved thought he was dead and buried, Shame wasn't sure what kind of reception would await him when he showed up out of the blue.

Though his family was in for a shock, there was little Shame didn't know about his wife and daughter. It was amazing what you could learn about someone over the web. It had been a few months since he'd last looked in on them, he'd been busy, but he knew all he needed. Their current address had long since been memorized. His wife hadn't remarried. And his daughter was a happy and healthy twelve-year-old.

Shame had a long drive ahead of him but with the windows rolled down and the rock-n-roll turned up, things had never looked better. He was on his way home.

God help anyone or anything that tried to stand in his way.

About the Author

Amanda Young spends her days basking in the sun by the seashore and her nights surrounded by dozens of serenading male strippers whose only desire is to make her happy.

Yeah, right.

In real life, my husband chases away all the hot men, right before asking me what I'm going to fix him for dinner and reminding me to do the dishes for the umpteenth time.

Always an avid reader of romance, I was thrilled when I discovered erotic romance. For a long while I toyed with the idea of writing my own but could never find the time.

When I found myself unemployed in 2006, I decided it was high time I gave it a shot. I sat down at my trusty computer and, according to my very patient husband, haven't moved since.

To learn more about Amanda Young, please visit www.amandayoung.org. Send an email to Amanda Young at amandasromance@aol.com

Look for these titles

Coming Soon:

Shameful
Taboo Desires
A Child's Love

Boxers or briefs?

Kiss and Tell
© 2007 Sandy Lynn

Willow is having a bad day. To get her sister to stop harassing her, she agrees to play a silly game—but only once. When a muscular hunk walks past her, Willow's mouth waters and she knows she's found the perfect man to ask her embarrassing question.

Seth is shocked when a beautiful woman sits on his lap. He's amused when she begins asking him questions. But he's aroused when she kisses him. Taking her back to his home, he sinks his teeth into her—and is addicted. Imagine his surprise when he finds out she holds his life in the palm of her hands.

What's a vampire to do when the woman he needs for his survival runs screaming from him?

Available now in ebook from Samhain Publishing.

Enjoy the following excerpt...

Willow watched in shock as Seth knelt on the elevator floor in front of her. Lifting her shirt, he kissed one erect nipple before shifting to the other, circling it with his tongue. Sucking the already tight bud into his mouth, he looked up into her face.

She knew desire was written all over her expression. How could it not be with the things he had done—was doing to her body?

A very low moan escaped her throat as he teased first one breast then the other. Her breasts ached with desire. She wasn't sure how much longer she could wait to feel him inside of her. Back and forth he altered his focus, making certain each breast received equally lavish attention.

After what felt like an eternity, the elevator finally stopped, bringing Willow back to reality once again. How was he able to make her lose herself so completely? Never before had she become so wrapped up in what was happening to her that she'd forgotten completely about her surroundings. Yet Seth had managed to make her forget everything but him twice that evening. What if there had been another stop, and another person—or couple—had joined them inside the small car?

Seth stood quickly and, without warning, picked her up. The feel of his arms so strong around her forced her to forget her previous embarrassment. He carried her through the apartment, not pausing to show her anything, but she didn't mind. She was too entranced with this man who wove such a spell on her that she didn't bother to look around and see what his home was like.

In what felt like a few short seconds, she was standing on her own again. Glancing around, she saw she was inside of his bedroom, by a bed that—when she turned to look at it—she noticed was decadently huge.

Watching him avidly, Willow felt her mouth water as Seth pulled off his shirt, revealing a well-muscled chest with just the right amount of hair covering it. She wouldn't feel as though she were in bed with a bear, but there was plenty for her to twist her fingers in as she enjoyed nibbling on his nipples. Sitting on the bed, Seth removed his shoes next. Willow looked back up at his face, desire still coursing through her. She was surprised to find his steady gaze on her, as though he were gauging her reaction to him.

Reason once again tried to intrude on her pleasure. *How did things get this far this fast? Is this really what I want?* Questions assailed her as she pondered the wisdom of allowing things to move so quickly. She wasn't used to jumping into one-night stands.

After the unbelievable orgasm he'd given her in the bar, surrounded by people, Willow was sure he was a talented lover. No one had ever made her feel that way while in a crowded room before. Never before had she been even remotely tempted to leave a bar with a man she had just met.

Her gaze feasted on what she could see of his bare body as he stood, and the sensible side of her wondered if she should put a stop to things before his mouth made her forget everything but him once more.

Her gaze followed the trail of soft brown hair leading down to the waistband of his jeans and she licked her lips. Seth paused, grasping the button, ready to open his pants or possibly to stop if she were to give the slightest protest.

Sensing his hesitation made her decision easier. Tonight she would forget she was the mature sister. Tonight she would be immature and selfish, taking what she wanted. And she wanted Seth. She gave herself permission to have fun and not to question every minor action, to do things that she would typically be entirely too embarrassed to try. Walking over to him, she eased his hands away from their position then unbuttoned his jeans herself as she rose to her tiptoes to place a tender kiss on his lips.

Pulling slightly away from him, she easily played the part of temptress when he tried to coax her into a deeper kiss. Tugging his jeans low, she felt them fall off of his hips. Taking a single step back, Willow admired the body now bared completely to her.

Her eyes widened as she stared at him. Having him beneath her, erect but still fully dressed, had not prepared her for just how blessed he was down there. He was huge! His cock was long, thick and hard, and it looked as if it were ready to attack.

His body is truly amazing. To let a body like this go to waste is shameful.

Stepping closer, she allowed her fingers to skim down his hard body. She was unable to feel so much as an ounce of spare fat on him. His muscles tensed beneath her light touch. Finally taking his erection into her hand, she stroked the velvety flesh while he looked down at her.

She felt powerful and seductive. A smile tilted Willow's lips. Lowering herself to her knees on the hardwood floor, she licked the single fat drop of moisture from the silky tip.

Seth's groan of pleasure encouraged her to continue. Guiding his cock to her lips, she traced the head with her tongue before sucking him into her mouth. She stroked him that way for a few moments, her tongue moving against the soft underside as he withdrew from her. Willow was careful to savor any moisture that escaped him. She whimpered when his hands stopped her ministrations.

"Ah, sweetheart, if you keep that up we'll both be disappointed," he told her. His voice was husky with desire as he pulled himself from her mouth while she pouted.

Pulling her up his body, Seth kissed Willow's bottom lip, taking it into his mouth, ruining her pout. When the kiss ended, her shirt was off and thrown somewhere—she believed it was across the room. Her shoes and miniskirt soon followed. She wasn't sure exactly how he managed to strip her so quickly, unable to process much of anything other than the assault on her senses. She wondered if the pleasure portion of her brain was being overloaded.

Seth picked her up once again, and crossed the remaining slight distance to his sinful bed. Seconds after he lowered her to the mattress, he joined her, his body pressing hers deeper into the soft bedding. He resumed his earlier teasing of her breasts, palming them as he kissed her deeply. Her hips arched against him and this time he was the one with a wicked grin. His mouth set a trail of fire coursing down her body everywhere it touched. She raised her hips, inviting him closer when he nipped her flesh. When she arched up, he winked at her before continuing his delicious torture. Willow was ready to end all games, to pin him to the bed, as her pussy ached to feel him buried deep inside of her.

Unmindful of how badly she wanted him at the moment, Seth seemed content to take his time. He slid his hand slowly up her leg, caressing her flesh before teasing and stroking her sex. Biting down on her lip, she closed her eyes and arched her hips as he slid his finger deep inside of her, and thrust gently.

"Oh, sweetheart, you're so wet. I want to taste you," he murmured, his head close to her pussy. The second the words left his mouth, his finger was replaced by his tongue.

He parted her folds, and allowed his thumb to circle her straining clit. Raising his mouth slightly, he pressed two fingers deep within her as he suckled the small bud into his mouth.

"You taste like honey." His breath wreaked havoc on her as it met her damp flesh.

She wasn't sure what exactly turned her on more; his words, his mouth or his fingers. What was it about him that made her lose control so completely? Never before had talking dirty made her this wet, but then everything Seth did to her—everything he said—made her want him more.

"Oh God." The moan escaped her as she felt herself straining, her muscles tensing when she felt another orgasm approaching.

"What would you like, sweetheart?" Seth sucked on her swollen bud once before continuing. "What do you want?"

"I want to feel you," she pleaded. "All of you inside of me. Please."

Discover eBooks!
THE FASTEST WAY TO GET THE HOTTEST NAMES

Get your favorite authors on your favorite reader, long before they're out in print! Ebooks from Samhain go wherever you go, and work with whatever you carry—Palm, PDF, Mobi, and more.

WWW.SAMHAINPUBLISHING.COM

Printed in the United States
89633LV00003B/234/A